A FAMILY AFFAIR

Borgo Press Books by Victor J. Banis

*The Astral: Till the Day I Die * Avalon: An Historical Novel * The C.A.M.P. Cookbook * The C.A.M.P. Guide to Astrology * Charms, Spells, and Curses for the Millions * Color Him Gay: That Man from C.A.M.P. * The Curse of Bloodstone: A Gothic Novel of Terror * Darkwater: A Gothic Novel of Horror * The Daughters of Nightsong: An Historical Novel (Nightsong Saga #2) * The Devil's Dance: A Novel of Terror * Drag Thing; or, The Strange Tale of Jackle and Hyde * The Earth and All It Holds: An Historical Novel * A Family Affair: A Novel of Horror * Fatal Flowers: A Novel of Horror * Fire on the Moon: A Novel of Terror * The Gay Dogs: That Man from C.A.M.P. * The Gay Haunt * The Glass House: A Novel of Terror * The Glass Painting: A Gothic Tale of Horror * Goodbye, My Lover * The Greek Boy * The Green Rolling Hills: Writings from West Virginia (editor) * Green Willows: A Novel of Horror * Kenny's Back * Life & Other Passing Moments: A Collection of Short Writings * The Lion's Gate: A Novel of Terror * Love's Pawn: A Novel of Romance * Lucifer's Daughter: A Novel of Horror * Moon Garden: A Novel of Terror * Nightsong: An Historical Novel (Nightsong Saga #1) * The Pot Thickens: Recipes from Writers and Editors (editor) * San Antone: An Historical Novel * The Scent of Heather: A Novel of Terror * The Second House: A Novel of Terror * The Second Tijuana Bible Reader (editor) * The Sins of Nightsong: An Historical Novel (Nightsong Saga #3) * Spine Intact, Some Creases: Remembrances of a Paperback Writer * Stranger at the Door: A Novel of Suspense * Sweet Tormented Love: A Novel of Romance * The Sword and the Rose: An Historical Novel * This Splendid Earth: An Historical Novel * The Tijuana Bible Reader (editor) * Twisted Flames * The WATERCRESS File: That Man from C.A.M.P. * A Westward Love: An Historical Romance * White Jade: A Novel of Terror * The Why Not * The Wine of the Heart: A Novel of Romance * The Wolves of Craywood: A Novel of Terror*

A FAMILY AFFAIR

A NOVEL OF HORROR

V. J. BANIS

THE BORGO PRESS
MMXII

A FAMILY AFFAIR

FIRST BORGO PRESS EDITION

Published by Wildside Press LLC

www.wildsidebooks.com

DEDICATION

I am deeply indebted to my friend, Heather, for all the help she has given me in getting these early works of mine reissued.

And I am grateful as well to Rob Reginald, for all his assistance and support.

CONTENTS

CHAPTER ONE 9

CHAPTER TWO 25

CHAPTER THREE 31

CHAPTER FOUR 43

CHAPTER FIVE 57

CHAPTER SIX 70

CHAPTER SEVEN 85

CHAPTER EIGHT 93

CHAPTER NINE 101

CHAPTER TEN 115

CHAPTER ELEVEN 129

CHAPTER TWELVE 134

CHAPTER THIRTEEN 145

CHAPTER FOURTEEN 151

CHAPTER FIFTEEN 160

CHAPTER SIXTEEN 169

CHAPTER SEVENTEEN 180

CHAPTER EIGHTEEN 191

CHAPTER NINETEEN 195

CHAPTER TWENTY 203

ABOUT THE AUTHOR 206

CHAPTER ONE

Her mother was dead. Panting with the exertion of what she had done, Jennifer Rand felt a perverse excitement. Slowly, with infinite caution, she removed the pillow that she had held so tightly against her mother's face and stared wide-eyed at the figure sprawled ungraciously over the bed.

Yes, she was dead, there could be no doubt of it. Jennifer's eyes filled with tears, her mouth worked wordlessly. She stood as though transfixed, the awesome warmth of the pillow clutched to her breast. Then, dropping it all at once, she turned full around and half-ran, half-danced from the room. She pirouetted through the living room, bursting through the kitchen and out into the moonlight that flooded the backyard. Her mother was dead. Dead. Dead.

"Jennifer?"

As a balloon bursts when punctured, so Jennifer's spirits burst, the exhilaration that had filled her spilled from her in one horrible rush.

"Jennifer?"

Sleep was rushing away from her, carrying with it the dream. Jennifer reached for them, tried to hold them to her, but the voice was too strong, instinct was more powerful than desire. She lay huddled and wearied in her small bed, and accepted waking with grim resignation.

"I'm here, Mother." She held her eyes closed, trying to recall the dream. It had been something pleasant, of that she was certain, although she could not remember what; but not altogether pleasant, for lingering with the sense of freedom and exhilaration was an eerie feeling of guilt. She concluded that she had been dreaming of something wicked, and wondered what on earth it might have been.

"I've been calling you." Her mother's voice was heavy with reproach and self-pity.

"I didn't hear you," Jennifer offered meekly. Then, as though to substantiate the claim, she added, "I was asleep."

"I called and called. I thought you had gone somewhere. You know I want you close by me."

The dream, where had it gone? If she closed her eyes and surrendered to her sleepiness, would it come back to her?

"Did you want something, Mother?" It was useless. She would have to begin all over the maddening ritual of begging sleep, coaxing her body and her mind into the realm of non-consciousness, gradually drifting and waiting for the dream to come for her again, in its own way and its own time. It would come. It had come before and gone, and although she could remember nothing about it, she knew that it was the same. Someday, she promised herself, I'll remember.

Her mother had not answered. Jennifer focused her attention in that direction, listening carefully. Yes, her mother was asleep again. She had wanted nothing after all, only to determine that Jennifer was here.

She'll want me to die with her, Jennifer thought bitterly, and at once flushed with guilt at the thought. What a dreadful thing to think, she scolded herself, and turned on her side, tugging the blanket up close about her chin.

She thought of her mother's medicine, sitting on the nightstand. She should have given it to her while they were both awake; it might have meant an opportunity for both of them to sleep comfortably past the time for it. But it was too late now. She would only have to awaken her mother, which would certainly provoke a quarrel, and in the end neither of them would get the advantage of the additional sleep.

"If only I weren't so tired," Jennifer thought wearily. "If only I could sleep."

But much sooner than she had expected, she fell asleep again.

"Jennifer?"

The voice was little more than a whisper as it penetrated the depth of Jennifer's slumber. A part of her, the wary sentry self, heard, and sounded its warning.

"Jennifer?"

From far, far away, Jennifer heard the warning. I should wake up now, she told herself, but the thought went unheeded. Sleep was so close about her, holding her tight in an embrace that would not be broken. And although the sentry listened throughout the night, the call was not repeated. Jennifer slept on without further intrusion upon her dreams.

****

Her mother was dead. Jennifer had known it when she first awakened in the morning. She knew it before she poured the medicine which was never taken, and she knew it without once touching the thin, wasted body. And when she called Doctor Blackstone to come at once, she did not say, "My mother is sick again," but very simply, "My mother is dead."

Doctor Blackstone's wife came with him.

In fact there was little either of them could do. Certainly the Doctor could only verify what Jennifer already knew to be true, that her mother was dead, and make arrangements for the body to be taken from the house. Nor was Mrs. Blackstone, determinedly cheerful creature that she was, any more effectual.

"You must let me take care of things for you," she insisted, fairly thrusting a cup of bitter smelling coffee into Jennifer's hands.

"Yes, of course," Jennifer agreed numbly, although for the life of her she could not imagine what there was to take care of.

"Are there any relatives I can contact for you?" Mrs. Blackstone asked. Her husband appeared briefly in the doorway, and she shooed him away with a wordless gesture. Jennifer heard him leave and guessed that his work was finished. It gave her a sense of finality. Death had come, and gone, and now it was finished. She let out her breath, and felt as if she had been holding it since she had first awakened and looked in the direction of her mother's bed.

"No, there aren't any relatives," she answered, and became truly conscious of the conversation for the first time since it bad begun.

There were no relatives. She had lived for as long as she could remember with her mother, the two of them alone. In the entire world, she knew of no one who should be notified, no one other than herself who cared if her mother was alive or dead.

"But surely your mother's family. There must be someone," Mrs. Blackstone persisted.

"I don't know," Jennifer admitted honestly and patiently. She was used to being patient, accustomed to hiding her resentments and private desires. Mrs. Blackstone was no match for her mother in trying the nerves. "There were relatives at one time. My mother's sisters, I think."

"Sisters, of course. Were there more than one?"

"I don't know," Jennifer said.

Mrs. Blackstone was growing visibly short of good cheer, but she pushed on. "Where are they living now?"

"I don't know that they are." Jennifer wished that she could help. She saw in Mrs. Blackstone's face the dreadful sense of uselessness that weighed upon her, and wished that she could relieve her of it, but she had spoken the truth. She knew nothing of her mother's family. At some time before she was old enough to remember clearly, they had lived with her mother's sisters. That much she did know, but she knew it from a few vague references that her mother had made over the years, and not from memory.

Why they had left, or why the ties had remained severed in the intervening years, she had never known. In all the years she had lived with her mother, Jennifer remembered no correspondence between the two branches of the family, nor communication of any kind, so that she could not even be certain now that she had not imagined it altogether, vague references and all.

"Your father?"

Jennifer shook her head without even bothering to answer. She was so tired. If only she could be alone, if only she could sleep. Her mother had told her she used sleep as an escape, the way other people used liquor or drugs. It was probably true. She would like to sleep right now, curled up into a ball; sleep, and have to think of nothing.

Her father she did not remember at all, although she made an effort now for Mrs. Blackstone's sake. "He is no longer with us," her mother had explained when Jennifer, as a child, had raised that question, and that ended the discussion.

"I don't remember my father," she said aloud. "He is no longer with us."

The task proved finally too much even for Mrs. Blackstone's insistent sympathy. "Well, I suppose there's not much I can do," she said. "If you like I'll stay with you for the day. It isn't wise to be alone too much during these times, they say."

Jennifer lifted her face wearily, her eyes seeking the other woman's, and she allowed her eyes to say the things she would never permit herself to express in words.

"No, I'll be all right," she said aloud, but the rest was as clearly communicated.

"I see," Mrs. Blackstone said, meeting that chilling gaze, and backing down in the face of it. "I see."

When she had gone, Jennifer carried the coffee to the sink and poured it down the drain. She did not like coffee, and she'd had to force herself to sip it to satisfy Mrs. Blackstone. She was accustomed to doing as others expected of her, rather than what she herself would have liked to do. Now she could begin to do as she wished.

She thought of the things Mrs. Blackstone had said, the questions she had asked, and with those questions weighing on her mind, she left the kitchen and made her way to the bedroom.

The bed was empty now, and the sheets had been carefully smoothed. The sight of that smooth bed gave her an unexpected shock. Her mother might well have risen as she did in the past, and gone for a morning walk. At any moment she might come in the front door, with her firm, bold step. For the tiniest fraction of a second, Jennifer had an unpleasant sinking in the bottom of her stomach.

But of course her mother had not gotten up and gone for walks in well over a year, nor would she ever do so again.

Jennifer stood at the door, taking in the room. Her own small bed was still unmade, a fact for which her mother would certainly have scolded her. For the moment however she did not think it mattered much. Later she would move her bed back into her own bedroom, where it had been before her mother's illness had necessitated an every night vigil.

Her mother's desk was locked, as it had always been. The key was in the dresser, in the top drawer on the right. Jennifer took it, scarcely able to suppress a sensation of guilt as she did so.

The key was forbidden to her. Never had she been allowed to open the desk of her own accord, nor see its contents except at a glance. Snooping, her mother would have called it, and even now Jennifer stood with the key in her hand for several long minutes before she crossed the room to the desk and unlocked its drop front.

The hinge creaked a warning as she lowered the wooden shelf, and feeling a renewed pang of guilt, she again hesitated, listening, perhaps for the sound of approaching footsteps, or a scolding voice. The house sat silently around her, and her guilt faded, pushed aside by another emotion; she had a sense of childish excitement, the thrill of forbidden pursuits. Even the musty scent of old papers, drifting upward, added to her anticipation, and she approached searching the desk with a new enthusiasm.

Her enthusiasm soon faded. The desk held little of interest after all, certainly nothing to justify the privacy that Elenora Rand had maintained with such resoluteness over the years. Jennifer found a deed to the property, free and clear, and bank books which revealed a comfortable balance. There were no letters, no family albums, no pictures, and no names or addresses of friends or relatives; none.

With a feeling of disappointment she closed the desk again. She held the key in her hand for a moment, studying it as if it might answer the questions she had. Then, from habit, she locked the desk and returned the key carefully to the precise same place it had held before in the dresser drawer. If her mother had happened to come back, and had looked in the drawer for the key, she would probably have never seen that it had been moved, and used.

No one came to look for the key.

* * * * * * *

The funeral was not, if the term could be applied, a successful one. The weather was unusually cold for so early in the fall. Had it not been for the cold weather, there might have been a few people from the town in attendance, if not for the sake of respect, then at least out of curiosity.

As it was, the undertaker had to hire pallbearers, although Elenora Rand had lived in the town for nearly thirty years before her death. The only non-official person present, in fact, was Jennifer herself. Mr. Peabody, the undertaker, took note of the fact that Jennifer shed not one tear when her mother's body was lowered into the ground, although he told his wife afterward that she had certainly looked sad enough.

When it was all over, Mr. Peabody offered to drive Jennifer home rather than back to the funeral parlor, as was his custom.

"Thank you," she said, "but I think I'll walk."

Since it was less than a mile from the cemetery to town, he left her without arguing the point, not a little relieved to be finished with this particular interment. As a general rule, he liked his work. He got to meet people. His customers, neither the living nor the dead, rarely argued with him. He saw himself as playing one of the fundamental roles in the scheme of things, in which he attended to the rounding off of the cycle, so to speak. He did not think of his bodies as dead people, because that to him was a contradiction in terms. People were alive, and these figures that he arranged so artfully in the coffins were only symbols, symbols of the completeness of life. And the burial was its final step, one which generally gave him a sense of satisfaction.

This burial gave him little satisfaction, and he resented Jennifer for it. "Peculiar," he described it to his wife afterward.

"They always were," she said.

Alone at the grave of her mother, Jennifer stared at the ground and at the coffin suspended just below ground level. Then, when the men arrived to complete the burial, she left and walked slowly across the cemetery, passing through the massive iron gates that opened onto the road.

She walked automatically, giving little thought to the town that approached and quickly surrounded her. It was a pretty town, as towns go, but she had long ago shut most aspects of the town out of her mind, the prettiness with the rest. She could pass through it now a hundred times without really seeing any of it.

The few people who saw her passing experienced very fleetingly a twinge of grief, which was forgotten almost by the time she had drifted by. It was not that the local people felt no sympathy for death; indeed, they did, and for the people left behind. But after all, the Rands had never been what you could call friendly. Everyone in town knew them by sight, but not more than a handful of people could honestly claim to have carried on any sort of conversation with Jennifer or her mother. And the reports of Doctor Blackstone and his wife had not helped further any sympathy for Jennifer.

"It's unnatural," Mrs. Blackstone had said to any available ear. She had, although she would not say this, never forgiven Jennifer for that one glance across the kitchen table, nor was she likely ever to do so. "The way that girl is taking it. Not a sign of grief, not the first human emotion to anything."

And the women to whom she spoke, as well as the men to whom the Doctor spoke, clucked their tongues and stayed their distance as Jennifer went by.

She was alone. It was this fact, more than the death of her mother, that saddened Jennifer. She was twenty-six, a slim pale girl who had already begun to think of herself as a spinster. She was pretty, in a frail sort of way, but she did not know it, because no one had ever told her. She had no suitors, nor friends of any kind— no one to whom she could turn now for consolation or companionship.

She knew that people regarded her as peculiar. Always, she had been kept at a distance from other people. As a little girl she had not been permitted to have friends. They had lived, she and her mother, very nearly as hermits, and by the time her first year at school had ended, Jennifer already knew that the other children thought her "funny," and made up little rhymes about her: "Jenny, Jenny, eat a daisy, Jenny, Jenny, you are crazy." It had made her withdraw, and cooperate in her mother's efforts to isolate them.

For twenty-six years her life had centered around her mother, that strong, demanding creature whose demands had finally ceased so abruptly. For years Jennifer had been not so much a daughter as a combination of companion and house servant, and later, of course, nurse. Her time and her energies had belonged not to herself but to Elenora Rand exclusively. Every mood, every notion, every whim had been at the request of, or merely a reflection of, the older woman. She had resented her role, and yet she had hidden her resentment and played it without complaint, because she had been trained to do just that.

She reached home, the simple white cottage she had lived in for as long as she could remember. It was neat and clean and thoroughly respectable. The shutters were closed over the windows, as they always had been.

Once again the sensation of aloneness came over her and Jennifer stopped, half frightened of entering the house. It held no welcome for her. It was where she had lived, it was now all she had or was in life; but it was not home to her uneasy spirit.

There was no place else for her to go. She climbed the three steps that led to the front door and entered the hall, with a quick furtive manner as if afraid someone might try to follow.

It was not until she had dutifully put her coat away in the closet and had gone into the kitchen to make herself a cup of tea that she remembered the letter. It had come the day before and, puzzled by it, she had put it aside to read it later when the bother and distraction of the funeral was over.

She went to her bedroom—not to her mother's room, where she had been sleeping on the little bed, but to her own bedroom, that she had returned to. The letter was in the drawer of her dresser, next to a strand of cultured pearls. She had ordered the pearls from a mail order catalog, and her mother had been angry when they came; but she had relented, and allowed Jennifer to keep them, "for special occasions." They had never been worn. Jennifer had considered wearing them to the funeral, but had not been able to decide on her own whether that was the right sort of special occasion, and in the end she had gone without them.

Jennifer took the letter back to the kitchen, but she did not read it until her tea was ready and she was seated at the small kitchen table. Then she opened it carefully and unfolded the single sheet of paper.

It was the opening line that most puzzled her: "Your mother asked us to write and...."

It was from someone who signed her name Aunt Christine. Strange, although Jennifer had searched her mother's personal papers more than once since the death, carefully examining every item in the small desk, she had found no trace of any relatives. And now here was this letter, signed Aunt Christine, and saying, "Your mother asked us to write and invite you to visit with us at Kelsey House."

Of course her mother had known for a year or more that she was dying; no doctor would have dared to conceal the fact from her. It was entirely possible that, in a flash of foresight, she had written to her sisters, those long neglected relatives, explaining that her daughter would soon be in need of family ties. And they of course had seen the obituary notice in the newspapers.

What was odd, though, was that they had made no attempt to attend the services, nor even to send flowers. Had they done even the latter, the single wreath that Jennifer had herself provided might not have looked so forlorn. There was not even an expression of sympathy in the letter, although perhaps that might be attributable to tact.

Jennifer tasted her tea, found it cool, and sipped it slowly. Since her mother's death she had been busy with funeral arrangements and putting affairs in order. The house was hers, with no entanglements, and the money in the bank was sufficient to provide for her modest needs. Her time was her own. For someone who had never known time of her own, that should have been a source of joy.

The fact was that it was not, though. Not until this very morning, with the funeral actually at hand, had she realized the absolute emptiness of her life. She had nothing at all to do with this sudden excess of time— no interests, no hobbies, no one to call upon, no job.

And now here suddenly was this latter, informing her that she did at least have a family. They were people she did not know, to be sure, and their behavior regarding her mother's death was peculiar to the point of bordering upon rudeness; but they were family nonetheless. What was even more important, they wanted her with them.

In the same moment, Jennifer realized what was an astonishing, even frightening fact. She missed her mother. After years of coolness, silence, even resentment, she suddenly wished that the house were again filled with that strong presence. For the first time she saw that it took two people to make any kind of relationship, even that of mistress and slave. Now she wanted someone to order her about, tell her what to do, occupy her time.

Her tea had grown cold. She carried it with her as she returned to the living room and seated herself at the desk there. She took a note, paper, and a pen from the drawer, and began to write in a neat, precise style.

"...I will very much enjoy an opportunity to visit with you at Kelsey. I will expect to arrive Thursday next, probably in the evening...."

She finished the note, reading it over several times before putting it in its envelope, and took it directly to the post office for mailing.

CHAPTER TWO

Jennifer leaned one shoulder against the door of her car and sighed wearily. Would there be no end to this day?

"Nope, no Kelsey place around here," the man outside the car window repeated for what seemed to her the hundredth time. She stared through the half opened glass at him impatiently, sniffing mentally at the stubble of gray beard and the blackened teeth that dominated his withered face.

If he says that one more time, I shall scream, she told herself, her customary patience wearing thinner with each passing moment. She took the letter from her purse, removing the folded sheet from its envelope.

"My aunt says that their home is here, near Hard Castle, and I'm sure she must know where she lives." Despite her annoyance, her voice sounded as calm as ever; it was the tone of voice one would use to address a stubborn child.

"And besides," she added, all but waving the envelope under his nose, "it's postmarked from Hard Castle."

"Ain't no Kelsey place around here."

It was like listening to a broken record. For a moment she considered her resolution to scream. Instead, she sighed despairingly and replaced the letter carefully in her purse. Turning the ignition key, she put the car in gear and, scarcely waiting for him to step back from the way, she drove angrily from the service station.

"Blast," she said aloud to no one. The letter from Aunt Christine had been so explicit in its direction for the drive, until it got her to Hard Castle. Why on earth should the instructions have petered out so weakly at this stage in the journey?

"Take Bellen Road off of Peters Road." That was all the letter said. There was nothing as to where Peters Road was in relation to Hard Castle, nor how far she went in what direction. And that old fool at the station had not only never heard of either road but he had insisted on contributing to her annoyance by telling her that the Kelseys did not live anywhere near here. For all she knew, the road she was looking for could be two states away, and in the opposite direction.

She chastised herself for being so irritable. In the past, she had controlled her emotions better. It was difficult for her to adjust to the fact that now she could not only feel what she wished, but she could express those feelings if she wished.

"Heavens," she thought aloud, "I sound as if I'm happy my mother's gone."

Her thoughts went back to the night of her mother's death; what was it about that night? Something about it haunted her, lingering just below the surface of her consciousness. Something that had happened, something perhaps that she had dreamed. Try though she might, however, she could not bring the thought to the level of consciousness.

Suddenly cross with herself for having pursued such thinking, she forced her attention to the present. The sun was sinking ever lower toward the horizon. She scanned the sides of the road, but there was nothing in sight. At the present rate, she might very well think of spending the night someplace, and there was no sign of a motel.

It had seemed, from Aunt Christine's directions, a simple enough drive, and she had few reservations about making the trip by herself, although she had never before traveled alone. She had been careful also to schedule her departure so that, she had thought, she would arrive at Hard Castle the same day. She did not like traveling at night, particularly in what was now proving to be rather unpopulated country.

Almost on cue, she saw a sign for Peters Road. She hit the brake, bringing the car to a stop just beyond the turn-off. Slowly and none too confidently, she backed the car up and made the turn on Peters Road.

It's no wonder, she thought, that the man at the service station never heard of this road.

The road was little used, if its present state of repair were any indication. Large chuckholes forced her to keep her speed to a crawl. Small stones banged against the underside of the car. Increasingly ill at ease, she glanced again to the side of the road, allowing the car to run straight through a particularly bad chuckhole.

Hands shaking, she brought the car to a stop. It was an older model car, one her mother had purchased new many years before. Without knowing much about automobiles, Jennifer nevertheless suspected that this one would not long endure the treatment it was getting on this road.

For a moment she considered returning to Hard Castle for the night and making her way to Kelsey House in the morning. The road, which had thus far offered no sign of habitation, was lined on either side by dense woods. The tall trees and the rapidly fading sunlight left her in a dark gloom. The thought of driving this road after sundown was anything but pleasant.

She looked along the road again. Scarcely more than one lane, it did not even afford room for her to turn the car around. In order to return the way she had come, she would first have to continue on at least until she found a driveway or a lane, or even a wide spot.

Jennifer started off again slowly. Her uneasiness grew as the woods crept by on either side of her car, offering no relief. By now the sun had disappeared behind the tops of the trees and she was obliged to flick on the headlights in order to see where she was going. In their dim glare she nearly missed a narrow lane that cut into the woods on her right.

With a sigh of relief, she turned the car into it and shifted into reverse. She was backed halfway around before the headlights picked up the sign, all but covered over with brush, that identified Bellen Road.

She hesitated, half on and half off the road. The drive back into Hard Castle would be an arduous one in the dark. What's more, there was no assurance of finding a place to stay once she reached the town. Hard Castle seemed to consist of little more than a main street. A general store and the service station at which she had stopped earlier were the only visible business establishments in the town. Certainly she had seen nothing even resembling a motel.

She was tired and she was hungry, and there was no assurance that Hard Castle could provide relief for either need. On the other hand, the drive on to Kelsey House surely could not be any more difficult than retracing her route, and there at least she was assured of dinner and some degree of hospitality.

Gritting her teeth, she shifted the gears again and turned onto Bellen Road. At least, she comforted herself, this road seemed to be an improvement over the one she had been traveling on previously. This was as narrow, true, and nothing more than dirt, but at least the dirt was solidly packed. In comparison to the last hour of driving, it seemed quite smooth.

She was able to drive faster now, watching to the sides of the road for some sign of a house, although as yet she had seen none.

The daylight was completely gone by this time. The twin beams of the headlights offered the only break in the blackness that surrounded the car. Jennifer's back had begun to ache from the unaccustomed driving, and her eyes were feeling the strain of staring steadily through the windshield. She gripped the wheel tensely as she steered the car around a curve that appeared before her. As she did so, the lights reflected back to her from the road ahead.

The seconds that it took for her to comprehend the meaning of that phenomenon cost her the distance in which she might have been able to stop the car. She had scarcely gotten her foot to the brake pedal before she hit the stream. A sheet of water dashed across the windshield, blinding her completely. Seized by panic, she felt the car slide out of control before it shuddered to a stop in the center of the stream.

For a long time she could only sit motionless, clenching the steering wheel tightly in her hands, and trembling. At last she said aloud, "Of all the fool things. You'd think they'd have heard of bridges, even here."

The sound of a voice, even her own, restored her to some semblance of calm. She pressed on the accelerator, and realized for the first time that the motor had stopped. Her attempt to start it again produced nothing more than a sputter and a whine. With each successive attempt, the whine grew fainter, descending in pitch. Finally, her efforts caused nothing but a clicking noise, and she realized that the battery was dead.

CHAPTER THREE

For a full moment she fought off the urge to throw her face into her hands and cry.

"Hysteria isn't going to get me anywhere," she insisted to herself, at the same time admitting that she was not sure just what was going to get her anywhere—certainly not her car. Cautiously she opened her door and peered out. The water was not very deep. At least she would not be trapped in her car, where she would have to wait for days to be rescued.

Just what was she to do, though? The business of making decisions was a new one for her, and one that she was not finding to her liking. In the past, her mother would have told her just what she should do, and probably it would have been exactly right for coping with the situation. It would certainly be easier if her mother were in the car just now to take charge.

"Well, she isn't here," she told herself angrily. Her annoyance with herself added to her annoyance with the journey and the irritation of finding herself stranded in the middle of a stream. With a determination fired by anger, she slipped off the low shoes she had worn for driving, dropping them into the oversize handbag beside her on the seat.

The water was icy cold on her bare foot, causing her to shudder involuntarily. With stubborn resolution, she grabbed her purse and slid off the seat, standing almost knee deep in the cold water. But despite its depth at this point, the water was slow-moving, and she was in no danger at all of being swept away in the current. She lifted her skirt and waded to the opposite side of the creek, nearly falling when she stepped on a slippery rock. She paused on the bank to put her shoes on and contemplate her predicament.

There was nothing for it but to leave the car and her luggage and start walking. Heaven alone knew how far she would have to walk before finding Kelsey House, or any other house for that matter. In the morning there would be time enough to worry about the car and her luggage. Surely there would be someone at Kelsey House to retrieve them for her.

She started stubbornly down the road. Without the comforting beams of the car's headlights, the road seemed darker. She found herself frighteningly aware of its narrowness and of the tall trees towering over her on either side, like threatening sentinels. The air was filled with the sweet scent of pine and sage and juniper. What had seemed at first to be silence was not silence after all, but a sighing of leaves and branches in the breeze, and the whisper of birds overhead. There was another sound too, a faint rustling in the underbrush that might have been the breeze again, or that might have been someone moving stealthily through the woods beside her.

She walked carefully down the middle of the road, casting frequent glances about. She remembered the stories she had read as a child, stories of roving bandits who hid in the forests and leapt out to accost unwary travelers.

"There aren't any roving bandits these days," she reminded herself aloud, without in the slightest allaying her fears. One could hardly live in the world today without being aware that there were all kinds of people just waiting to do horrible things. And for all she knew, in a place so forlorn and isolated as this, where they did not even know enough to put bridges across streams, there might just still be roving bandits.

The road sloped uphill, leveling off just before it disappeared around another curve. She reached the flat ground again and began to walk more swiftly. The determination that had carried her away from the car had been more than anything else a product of her anger. As her distance from the relative comfort of the car increased, she found both her anger and determination waning.

She was halfway around the curve when she saw the man standing in front of her, a short distance down the road. She stopped dead in her tracks, fighting the temptation to turn and run. There could be no doubt of it, he had seen her; he was, in fact, watching her.

"Don't be a ninny," she told herself without much resolve. You've been wanting to see some sign of life and unless there's some horrible mistake, this certainly is one.

"Hello," she called aloud, not moving from the spot where she stood. "Can you direct me to Kelsey House?"

There was such a long pause before he answered that she half wondered if he had heard her at all, and was about to call again when he finally spoke.

"You must be Miss Jennifer," he called back, quite as though she had just opened the door of her home to find him there waiting to greet her, rather than having met him along an isolated country road at night.

The fact that he knew her name startled her at first. It was an incongruous spot in which to find someone who could address her by name.

"Miss Kelsey said I should bring you up to the house," he went on as he drew nearer.

Jennifer let out the breath she had been holding in a great sigh of relief. Of course, she chided herself for her stupidity. He was a servant that her aunt had sent out to watch for her. After all, they did know she was coming, they were expecting her, and she was considerably later than she had indicated in her letter. They had grown concerned, which was nice to realize, and had sent this man out to see if anything had happened to her.

"Oh, thank Heaven," she said aloud. "I had all but given up hope of ever finding the place."

"She thought you might need some help. People coming from outside can't see the place without help," he said.

"It must be very isolated," she said, thinking his

remark strange. But the trees around her were very high and thick, and she could well understand that a house would be difficult to spy if it were shielded from the road.

The man had stopped directly in front of her, studying her intently but with no sign of either pleasure or displeasure at what he saw.

"Are you Mr. Kelsey?" Jennifer asked. He did not act very much like a servant. She had not, as it were, had much experience in such matters, but he did not act as she would expect a servant to act; not even, she thought fleetingly, as she had acted toward her mother.

The man chuckled, a fact which Jennifer regarded as rude. There was not, so far as she could see, anything humorous in her question.

He grew abruptly sober. "No," he said. "Mrs. Kelsey did him in a long time ago."

What exactly did one say to such a comment, Jennifer wondered? He was a strange one, that was for sure. Under any other circumstances, she would probably have brought him down a peg or two. Unfortunately, this was neither the time nor the place to take exception with his manners. He was not Mr. Kelsey, but he might be a relative, or a friend of the family; or he might, after all, prove to be a servant, and a very rude one. Whatever he was, she promised herself, she would inform her aunt of his peculiar remarks and his rather rude manner. It was hardly what ought to be due a guest who had just arrived, and was in addition a stranger here.

Since he had made no attempt to indicate the way, she asked, "Is it far to Kelsey House?" She had spent quite enough time on this silly road for one night, and was eager now to be at her destination.

"No, we'll take the path," he said. "Save some time." He turned and started toward the woods.

She had seen no sign of a path, and her first thought was that he was somehow mistaken. But when she looked in the direction that he was going, sure enough she saw a break in the denseness of trees and shrubs. There was no question that it was a path, quite a well used one, leading sharply off from the road. It was strange that she had not noticed it before; but then, she reminded herself, she had not really been looking for a path so much as for some sign of the house itself—a mailbox, perhaps, or the sight of lights burning in the distance. Those things were still not in evidence.

"Oh, I say," she called after him, suddenly remembering how she happened to be walking along here, and not driving her car. "I left my luggage back in the car. It stalled back there in the stream. I wonder if you would mind getting it out for me?"

"Your car?" he asked rather skeptically, pausing without looking back.

"Oh, no, I meant the luggage. It's in the car." What an annoyingly dense creature he was.

"What's in it?" he asked, still without turning.

The man was not only dense, but impertinent as well. "In my luggage? Why, my clothes of course," she answered, restraining herself with an effort.

His answer was unintelligible to her, little more than a grunt, and he started off again toward the woods. She opened her mouth to insist and then closed it again. Alone, in the middle of the night and the middle of nowhere, she was not really in much of a position to argue with this strange man.

In any event it would probably be better to let Aunt Christine handle the matter. She resolved again that Aunt Christine would be sure to learn all this as soon as they reached the house. She knew that if her mother were around, this would be quickly straightened out. Well, she would put the whole business in her aunt's hands, just as if Aunt Christine were her mother.

She followed the man into the woods. The darkness enveloped them. Jennifer found that she had almost to run to keep up with her guide. Once, when she stopped to free her skirt from an extending branch that had caught hold of it, he went on until she had lost sight of him altogether.

"Wait," she called after him, literally tearing the fabric loose from the branch that held it. To her greater annoyance, the man went on, and she had to run to catch up to him again. He did not seem to slow his pace at all. She was furious, and only years of keeping her emotions firmly in check enabled her to keep from speaking her mind.

She could not say how far they had come through the woods. They seemed to hurry forever through the dark dampness. She was tired and unhappy, and the journey took on an unreal dreamlike quality. The trees they hurried past seemed to be moving, coming to life. She felt she had crossed from one world and time into another. Time moved at a different pace. Her watch, when she paused to glance at it, seemed to be moving faster and faster. She thought, this is what it feels like to die.

The suddenness with which they left the woods and emerged onto the lawn of Kelsey House was startling. One moment they were surrounded by the dense growth and the awesome darkness. The next moment they were at the edge of a sweeping green and in the distance the house stood framed against the sky, its windows gleaming brightly. There was an eerie glow to the scene, which seemed to come not so much from the moon, now rising, but from things themselves, as if she were seeing the very essence of them.

It was a shock to be there so suddenly, to see the house stark and singular before them. But there was more to the scene than that alone. Between where she stood and where the house stood, a group of ghostly figures danced what might have been a child's game, or even a primitive rite of some sort. They twirled about in a circle, breaking free to spin wildly one at a time. There was the same eerie glow to the white, gauzelike gowns that they all wore; it made them look ghostlike.

The most shocking thing of all, to Jennifer's way of thinking, was that the gauzelike robes were all they were wearing. For all practical purposes, the women, for this they clearly were, were naked.

The dance came to a sudden stop, as if the music had

ended, although Jennifer had heard no sound of music. She decided it was her appearance that had made them stop, because they all turned toward her. There was an air of uncertainty, of confusion about them. For a moment they stood in silence, staring across the lawn at her. Finally one woman left the group and walked swiftly toward Jennifer. Rather, Jennifer found herself thinking, it was as if the woman floated across the lawn rather than walked. Again Jennifer had that odd sense of unreality, as if she were in a dream.

"Jennifer," the woman called as she came near. "I'm your Aunt Christine."

Jennifer took the extended hand stiffly. It was difficult to avoid staring at the strange creature who had greeted her. Even disregarding her peculiar garb, Aunt Christine was a singular individual. She was tall and willowy, and old—the lines about her mouth and eyes, the silver gray hair gleaming seemingly from within, gave evidence of that fact. Yet there was something about her that denied age, a childlike quality difficult to define but unmistakable nonetheless. It was almost as if she were in fact a very young person made up to appear very old; as if she were playing a role.

"I'm so happy to be here," Jennifer returned the greeting, aware that her voice lacked enthusiasm. She was not at all sure that she was happy to be here. "I hope I'm not interrupting anything," she added, unable to resist another glance at the strange little group of women who waited in the distance.

"Not at all," Aunt Christine said, quite unembarrassed by the scene. "We were nearly finished anyway, to tell the truth, and I'm sure they can manage the rest without me."

"What...." Jennifer hesitated. "What were you all doing?"

"Doing? Why, we were dancing, of course." Aunt Christine looked somewhat surprised. Then, abruptly, her expression changed, as if she had just remembered something. "Did your mother tell you anything about us?"

Jennifer shook her head. "Nothing at all. I didn't even know you existed until I got your letter. I thought I was alone in the world."

Aunt Christine had been studying her intently as she spoke, but now the older woman's face broke into a smile again, and she seized Jennifer's arm tightly. "Never mind about that, you aren't alone, and never will be again, I promise you," she said. "You're going to stay with us forever. But just now I'm sure you must be exhausted, and listen to me chattering away like a magpie. Let's just the two of us go on up to the house, and you can meet the others a little later."

They started toward the house on a course that took them safely past the group of women. Glancing again in their direction, Jennifer saw that the dancing had been resumed; they twirled and swayed, moving in a circle upon the grass. The white of their robes twirled after them, like tendrils of mist.

"Would you mind awfully," Jennifer asked in a weak voice, "asking them to put some clothes on?"

"Oh of course," Aunt Christine said with a little laugh. "We wouldn't go around the house like that."

I wouldn't go anywhere like that, Jennifer thought to herself. Aloud, she murmured a faint, "Of course."

Kelsey House and its inhabitants were certainly a far cry from anything she might have imagined. She was beginning to suspect that there might have been very good reasons why her mother had severed the family ties and left them severed all those years. Aunt Christine had implied as much, asking if Jennifer's mother had told her about them; what was there to tell, exactly?

Like it or not, though, she was here, and she had no intention of leaving before morning. She was exhausted; it was an effort to walk alongside Aunt Christine toward the house, and her eyelids felt as if they were made of lead. If nothing else, she was entitled to a night's rest. For that matter, she had no alternative. Without a car, in the dark, she could scarcely consider leaving, even if she had any place to go.

"We didn't wait dinner," Aunt Christine went on, "because I was afraid you might be late, but I've kept some warm for you. And I know you're tired. There's plenty of time to meet the others in the morning, if you'd rather."

"Yes, I think I would rather, thank you," Jennifer replied. Somehow she did not quite feel up to any more surprises for one day. She had had a long and tiring drive, climaxed with stalling her car in a stream. She had been frightened and then irritated by the man on the road—who, she observed now, seemed to have disappeared altogether. Then had come that strange journey through the woods, seeming to belong to no part of time or the world. And finally she had arrived at Kelsey House to finds its inhabitants engaged in some strange rite the significance of which she could not begin to guess.

She wanted no more surprises. What she did want, and all that she wanted, was a soft bed to stretch out on, and hour after hour of deep, restful sleep. Even food, although she had not eaten for several hours, was less important to her than the prospect of a night's sleep.

I hope, she thought a bit uneasily, their sleeping habits are a little less peculiar than some of their other habits.

CHAPTER FOUR

Kelsey House was like nothing that Jennifer had seen before. Its design defied classification, borrowing freely and without apparent purpose from every conceivable source. The entrance, which they approached now, was reminiscent of the plantation houses of the old South that Jennifer remembered from picture books; yet in this illusion the designer had failed. The porch was too small for that, all but devoured by the massive columns and the wide, sweeping stairs. Nor did the Victorian door with its ornate and multi-colored glass panels seem to belong to this setting.

From the porch the house flared out in either direction, not straight at all as one might expect, but at peculiar angles. It was as though the house were folding its wings about the front lawn. Here a turret, there an arch, elsewhere a gable—gestures that in the hands of a true artist might have been grand but succeeded here in being only grotesque.

"It's a strange house," Jennifer said. "I don't think I've ever seen anything quite like it."

Aunt Christine chuckled, a light, silvery sound. "Robert Kelsey designed it himself, and built a great deal of it with his own hands. He was a talented man, although not too artistic, I'm afraid, but he wanted it to express himself and his life. He traveled a great deal, in the old country, and in our own South, before the war. I think the house reflects those travels of his—rambling, seemingly without direction, and yet tied together with a certain power; determination, if you will."

"He must have been a fascinating man," Jennifer said.

"He was. You would have liked him."

Jennifer was not so sure of that. She knew all about strong willed people, and she knew that they could be fascinating without being at all likable.

They had come into the house. "I'll just dress," Aunt Christine said. "Why don't you have a seat in the parlor and I'll join you in a moment."

With a fluttering movement of her hand in the direction of what was presumably the parlor, Aunt Christine moved off down the hall. For a fleeting instant Jennifer felt the fleeting urge to go after her. She suddenly did not want to be alone, and especially not here, in this long, gloomy tunnel of a hall.

"Don't be a goose," she said under her breath. She turned to the room Aunt Christine had indicated, and entered through the partially open door.

She meant to sit down and was half into a small divan when, with an astonished gasp, she jerked herself upright again. The divan was filthy, covered with a thick layer of dust that did not appear to have been disturbed for years. With a shudder of disgust she quickly stood up, telling herself she would remain standing rather than suffer that kind of dirt.

When she looked about she saw that the entire room was in the same condition. Nothing was out of place, there was no sign of litter, but everything was covered with an accumulation of dirt and dust. Parlor or not, the room was clearly one that the family had not used for years, from the look of it It looked like a room that though fully furnished, had been abandoned long before, and since then disturbed by no human presence.

Aunt Christine coughed politely behind her. Turning, Jennifer caught her breath sharply in surprise. She had expected by this time to see her hostess clad in some more conventional style of clothing. Apparently, however, "dressing" meant nothing more to Aunt Christine than adding a filmy flowing gown of the same white gauze over the outfit she had been wearing.

"Would you like to eat in your room?" Aunt Christine asked, taking no apparent notice of Jennifer's surprise. "I'm sure you'll want to refresh yourself and I thought perhaps you'd rather be by yourself for a while."

"I certainly would," Jennifer thought. Aloud she said, "Yes, I'd like that."

"Come along then, I'll just show you to your room, and leave you there."

Dutifully Jennifer followed her aunt back to the hall they had entered a few moments before. It was a grim and curious entrance to the house, a long scantily lighted passageway that stretched gloomily before them. Above them the high, elaborately paneled ceiling was trimmed with ornate moldings down almost to the floor. The walls were lined with a seemingly endless stream of doors, all of them closed just now. The far end of the hall, toward which they now walked, was completely dominated by a wide, towering staircase.

And everywhere that Jennifer looked she saw the same dust that had so astonished her in the parlor. It was a puzzling and unpleasant sight, giving the impression that the entire house had been closed up and unused for years. Kelsey House, she told herself, was certainly in need of a good cleaning.

"How long have you been here?" she asked impulsively. It was entirely possible, after all, that the house actually had been closed up; the family might have just returned from traveling. That would even explain their peculiar absence from the funeral.

"Oh dear," Aunt Christine replied, "I lost count ever so long ago. It must be a hundred years now, I suppose, or even two hundred."

Jennifer frowned as she considered the reply. She had not intended the question to mean how long the family had been in residence, which apparently was how Aunt Christine had taken it, but rather how long Aunt Christine herself had been here.

She nearly explained this to her aunt, but restrained herself. For one thing, she was a guest in the house, and however peculiar she thought these people, it would hardly be appropriate for her to risk offending her hostess so soon after her arrival. Moreover, these peculiar people were after all her family, the only family she had.

And lastly, she was simply not accustomed to expressing her opinions, or to arguing a point. She would have to be patient, that was all; and patience was a virtue that she was well practiced in.

She did think, though, that she ought to try to make conversation, and besides, it was hard not to think of dozens of questions that one would like to ask about this strange place.

"What about the lights," she asked, noticing them. "They couldn't be as old as all that."

"Oh no, your mother's sisters added the lights and the plumbing, and did quite a bit of remodeling. Such a shame too."

"A shame?"

"Yes, they had only finished the work when the house burned to the ground."

That was certainly another confusing answer. Jennifer thought for a long moment, wondering if further questions along these lines would be rude. And if not, which piece of information should she question first. Every answer that she got from her aunt, far from satisfying her questions, only seemed to provoke further questions.

"Aren't you my mother's sister?" she asked finally, deciding to take things in the order they had been presented to her.

Aunt Christine's laugh sounded over her shoulder as they started up the wide staircase. "Heavens, I was your—let me see now—your great-great-grandmother's sister. I suppose I should have been more explicit in my letter, but the years have diminished my vanity very little. I think Aunt Christine makes me sound quite old enough, without adding the rest."

It was pointless, Jennifer thought to ask about the house burning to the ground. Aunt Christine might be teasing her, or perhaps her aunt was just not quite right mentally, not a very pleasant thought. In any event the answers she was getting were not making much sense.

"This is your room," Aunt Christine said. They had reached the second floor and turned to their left. The door that Aunt Christine indicated was the first in another long line of doors, again all closed.

Half frightened at what she might find, half hopeful, Jennifer turned the knob and pushed the door inward. Her hopes sank and faded. The room was every bit as dirty and uncared for as the rest of the house. Worse, even had it been clean, it would still have been a dismal-looking chamber.

The walls were covered with what she was certain, was the worst paper she had ever seen. At one time no doubt the red of the cabbage roses had been quite vivid. With the passing of time they had taken on a faded musty hue that was almost overpowering in its sense of agedness. The same paper stretched over the ceiling as well, giving one the impression of being smothered in an avalanche of paper flowers.

From the papered ceiling, although strangely not from the center of the room, hung a grotesque light fixture. It held three uncovered bulbs that glared harshly. Each light was held by the figure of a woman in flowing robes, not unlike those worn by the women on the lawn, or worn by those old Greek statues she had seen in pictures.

These were no innocent maidens, however, no happy women. Each of the three was frozen in a grotesque position, each face a study in horror and pain, a pain that would last through centuries, until the metal of which they were cast would return again to dust

Jennifer pulled her eyes away from the light fixture, shuddering a little involuntarily. The furnishings in the room were sparse and uninviting: a sprawling fourposter, a flowered comforter stretched across its surface, dominated the room. There was as well an old fashioned dresser, heavily carved, with its mirror set lopsidedly atop the dusty surface; a massive armoire that occupied one wall; and between the armoire and the bed a small stool. The single window was all but covered from sight by velvet drapes, and the floor was wood, stained to a somber blackness that fitted the overall dreariness of the room.

"I think you'll be comfortable here," Aunt Christine was saying from behind her. If she had noticed Jennifer's dismay, she gave no sign of it, and Jennifer kept her thoughts to herself.

"And I see Aunt Abbie has brought your dinner up," Aunt Christine said.

Jennifer followed her glance to the dresser, wondering how she had failed to notice the tray before.

In sharp contrast to the rest of the room, or the rest of the house for that matter, the tray and its silver cover gleamed brightly, clean and sparkling.

"I'll leave you to yourself now," Aunt Christine went on. "If you need anything, just let me know." With that she was gone, closing the door softly behind her.

"I'm alone," Jennifer told herself, staring unhappily about. "Alone in this nightmare of a room, in this peculiar house, miles from anywhere."

She shut her eyes and tried to remember just exactly where she was. She had left home at eight that morning and she had taken the highway north. The names of one or two towns stayed in her memory but they did little to make the picture any clearer. She was not accustomed to traveling, and furthermore she had virtually no sense of direction. Of course there was Aunt Christine's letter in her purse. At least with that she could always find her way back simply by reversing the directions.

If she went back. That was the rub. Put in the baldest terms, she had nothing to go back to; an empty house that held little appeal for her, and an emptier life. Kelsey House and its occupants seemed strange to her, that was true enough; but then, she herself had always been regarded as strange. It was possible that there were reasonable explanations for everything she had observed here. This was a large house, and it was possible that the family just did not try to keep it all clean.

That dancing on the lawn—well, it looked peculiar

to her, but it might be quite harmless. Suppose someone who knew nothing of the game happened upon a group of people playing charades; that would look peculiar too.

She must be patient. As for the house and its dirt, she could begin by taking the initiative and beginning a good cleaning-up job. Perhaps they would follow her example. With a lot of work, and soap and water, and maybe some paint, the house could be made—she paused in her thoughts and glanced around again—well, not charming, but at least more comfortable.

She would be very patient with Aunt Christine and the others. "They will come to like me," she said, "and to respect me." That thought raised her flagging spirits a little.

Her shoulder had begun to ache, and she was reminded that she was quite tired. She crossed to the bed, examining it with a feeling of revulsion. With two fingers she grasped one corner of the spread gingerly and pulled it to the foot of the bed. The sheets, protected by the spread, were relatively clean.

"That's something to be grateful for," she thought. At least she could have her sorely needed sleep; in the morning she would set herself to cleaning the room thoroughly.

The window was next. She tried without success to draw the drapes aside. Giving up on that attempt, she stuck her head behind the heavy velvet and tugged at the window, hoping to get at least a faint breath of fresh air into the musty room. The window refused stubbornly to budge. Still more disconcerting was the discovery that her hands were covered with the black dust that was thick on the windows.

"Oh dear," she said. She gave up on the window and stepped back into the room. It probably hadn't been opened since the fire, whenever that had been.

Her eyes fell on the silver tray still waiting atop the dresser. For a moment she played with the idea of going straight to bed without eating. She was more tired than hungry. Indeed, her very surroundings discouraged an appetite.

She was a creature of routine, however, and common sense told her finally that, hungry or not, she should try to eat a little something. She picked up the tray and turned around once or twice looking for a logical place to eat. There was none. Only the little stool and the bed offered any seating. Resignedly she carried the tray to the bed, setting it down in the middle of the uneven surface, and seated herself beside it. She removed the cover.

Beneath its silver cover, the tray was empty. Not really empty; neatly arranged on its surface was an assortment of dishes, cups, tableware, even a neatly folded napkin. But the dishes and the various containers were empty. Not one scrap of food marred their rather astonishing cleanness.

"Oh," she said aloud; and again, "Oh."

She rose from the bed, starting impulsively across the room, then came to an abrupt halt.

Perhaps they really were mad. Or perhaps, as seemed

more likely, this had been intended as a joke. She had a great deal of experience with that, ranging back to her childhood. The other children had often teased her in such a fashion, encouraging her with friendly gestures to do things that afterward were revealed as foolish, so that they could laugh at her. Funny Jenny, they had called her, and not only behind her back.

And for all she knew, the family was waiting for her somewhere, downstairs, or even just out in the hall. If she went marching out in search of Aunt Christine, she would give them their opportunity to have a good laugh at her expense.

There was the possibility too, she tried to console herself, that it was not a joke at all, but an honest mistake. There were reasons enough to suspect that the inhabitants of Kelsey House were a little eccentric. Aunt Whoever-it-was who had delivered the tray might simply have forgotten to put the food on it, in which case she would only be making a scene by protesting and making herself unpleasant.

"It can wait until morning," she said firmly. She removed the tray once again to the dresser. After all, she really wasn't hungry. In the morning, after a good night's rest, she would politely mention the matter of the tray to Aunt Christine, and no doubt there would be a perfectly logical explanation for it.

With a renewed if slightly less firm patience, she began to undress. She put her simple gray suit in the armoire on the single hanger that had been provided there, making a mental note that she would have to ask for more hangers.

The light switch was on the wall across the room and by the door, with the result that she stubbed her toe on the stool trying to find her way back to the bed. She stood still for a minute or two, allowing her eyes to adjust to the darkness. Amazingly enough, the small opening provided by the drapes did allow a bit of moonlight to filter into the room through the dusty window. After her pause, she was able to make her way to the bed without further mishap.

She pulled the sheet up to her chin, uncomfortable without her flannel nightgown. Despite her discomfort, however, and a day that had been trying on the nerves, her exhaustion had its way with her. She fell quickly into a deep and dreamless sleep.

She awoke with a start. For a moment the room and the bed were unfamiliar to her. It came back to her finally—the long drive and its conclusion. She was at Kelsey House, as a house guest. It was the middle of the night and something had awakened her. Someone had called her name; no, that wasn't possible, surely. She had dreamed it.

She peered into the darkness, her eyes slowly becoming adjusted to the darkness and the sudden awakening. She made out the dresser and the armoire, and the stool.

A movement from the direction of the hall door caught her eye. There it was again—faint, billowy, a white robed figure. With a tightening in her chest, she realized that there was someone in her room, someone in white who moved with maddening slowness toward her bed.

She lay motionless, her breath held in tightly. For the first time it occurred to her that she might be in some danger, alone with a houseful of people she did not know, who from all indications were far from normal. It was this thought that kept her from speaking out, from demanding to know who was there. She clutched the sheet tightly in her hand, watching through half closed eyes as the figure in white drew nearer. She could make out the form now of a woman—long dark hair falling about the shoulders, hands outstretched toward the bed. The face was in shadow.

Should she speak, Jennifer thought, demand an explanation for the intrusion? Or wait to learn the identity of her visitor. Or perhaps she should leap from the bed, make ready to defend herself?

Her teeth clenched to keep them from chattering, she closed her eyes, just as she had done when as a little girl she had been frightened in the darkness. Maybe whoever was here would go away. Maybe it was only a bad dream. If she pretended to sleep, it would just leave, surely.

The seconds crawled by. Frozen with fear, she listened for some sound, some indication of what was happening. The house lay silently about her. The room itself seemed to be waiting, listening.

Why was there no noise? Had her visitor, as she hoped, gone away?

A hand brushed lightly against her face, a hand

soft and so cold that it seemed to stop the blood in her veins. Jennifer nearly screamed. She bit sharply into her lip to stifle the cry that rose in her throat. Her body trembled and shook, seized by an inexplicable chill, and she felt a warning turn in her stomach.

Oh God, she thought, I'm going to be sick.

CHAPTER FIVE

The touch of that icy hand was brief, and did not
come again. The room remained silent. At last, unable
to contain herself any longer, she bolted to a sitting position, her eyes springing open. The room was empty!
She was alone!

She stared about in confusion and fright, doubting
her own senses, but the room was really empty. She
pinched herself once to determine that she was awake.

With the diminishing of her fear, she became
suddenly angry.

"That is the limit," she said aloud, not caring if
anyone heard. She almost hoped they did hear, in
fact, even if it did hurt their feelings. She was not
accustomed to having strangers parading through her
bedroom, pawing over her, to say nothing of frightening her to death.

Bounding noisily from the bed, she marched across
the room to the door and switched on the light. The
lock in the door was complete with key. She turned it
angrily, locking herself in, and any intruders out. So
much for moonlight visitors. Aunt Christine would
hear about quite a few things in the morning, and if

she offended them that was just too bad. There was a limit to what they could expect a person to tolerate without complaint

She reached for the light switch; then, changing her mind, she left the light burning and returned to bed. At least if there were anything further in store, she would not be in the dark.

This time it took longer for her to go to sleep. She listened for a time, thinking that her visitor might return and try the door, in which case she would tell someone a thing or two without waiting for morning.

As it happened, though, there was no further disturbance. At length she fell asleep, this time rather fitfully.

When she awoke again, it was morning. And her visitor had returned. At least, there was someone in her room. An elderly lady, looking older even than Aunt Christine, stood by the dresser. A tiny, birdlike creature with silver white hair and sparkling blackbird's eyes, the woman was humming to herself, a sad, hauntingly familiar melody. She wore the same peculiar white robes that Aunt Christine had worn the night before and her hands, like twin doves in flight fluttered about in the air over an empty vase on the dresser.

"Oh, good morning," the stranger greeted her when she saw Jennifer's open eyes. "I hope I didn't startle you."

"Yes, you did," Jennifer said, and at once wondered sleepily if she had been too blunt. The memory of her nightly intrusion came back to her then, and with that memory came some of her previous annoyance. "Not nearly so much as you did last night" she added, more sharply.

"Oh, did I see you last night? Were you on the lawn for the rites?"

"The rites?" It took Jennifer a moment to grasp the fact that the woman was referring to the strange goings-on she had seen on the lawn when she arrived.

"No, I was not," she replied coolly.

The stranger took no apparent notice of the coolness.

Her hands, as she spoke, continued to flutter about the empty vase, tugging at the air, patting it.

"Well then I couldn't have seen you last night. I left the rites early, only because Aunt Christine told me it would be all right, mind you. Let me see—oh yes, then I brought a dinner tray up here. After that I went straight to bed. I always retire early."

Jennifer hesitated to argue the matter. There was not really any evidence that it had been the same woman in her room the night before, and perhaps she was rash to make that assumption. They all seemed to wear the same robes. Better to take that matter up with Aunt Christine who, so far as she knew, was the mistress of the household.

Nonetheless, it was certainly disconcerting to find people wandering in and out of her room at will.

"How did you get in here?" she asked, suddenly remembering the locked door.

"Through the door," her visitor answered, quite as though it should have been obvious to anyone. As indeed, Jennifer told herself, it should have been. She opened her mouth to point out that the door had been locked, but her visitor interrupted her before she could mention it.

"Heavens, here I am chattering away with you," the woman said, "And I haven't even told you who I am. I am your Aunt Abbie." She beamed as though this bit of information should make everything quite clear.

"I see," Jennifer said, and, after a pause, she asked, "If it's not too rude of me, what on earth are you doing with that vase?"

"Why, I'm arranging the flowers. They're from my garden, you know. Aunt Christine says that no one can do as well with flowers as I do."

Jennifer looked again at the vase, then slowly about the room. If there were any flowers in the room, they could only be hidden under her bed. For a brief second she almost leaned out of the bed to look under there.

Now I'm beginning to act as oddly as they do, she chided herself.

"I'm especially pleased with the roses this year," Aunt Abbie went on proudly, giving a final tug at one of the unseen roses. "I don't know when I've seen such colors. There, I think that will do. I thought that you might appreciate some fresh flowers in your room when you awoke, and Aunt Christine said it would be all right. I hope you don't mind."

Jennifer was on the verge of telling her, manners or no, that she did mind, but again she was interrupted before she could begin.

"I almost forgot, I brought a robe for you," Aunt

Abbie said, pointing to the foot of the bed.

That much at least was real. There, draped neatly across one corner of the bed was another of the peculiar robes that seemed to be the uniform of the household. Jennifer poked it with her foot.

"That's very kind of you," she replied, making an effort to sound grateful. "But I think I'll manage with the things I've brought. I don't suppose the caretaker has fetched my luggage yet?"

"Why, we have no caretaker."

Jennifer sighed and spoke as she would speak to a child. "Well, whoever he was, the point is, I would like my luggage. Has anything been done about it?"

"Your luggage?"

"Never mind. I'll take it up with Aunt Christine," Jennifer said. This conversation was plainly getting her nowhere. "What time is breakfast?"

"Just as soon as you're up," Aunt Abbie said, looking pleased to have finished with the subject of the luggage. "But don't you rush any now. We'll be there whenever you're ready."

Jennifer did smile; it was maddening trying to talk to Aunt Abbie, but she was sweet, and she did seem genuinely eager to please. Aunt Abbie went out, closing the door gently after herself.

When she was alone, Jennifer remembered that she had not asked about the lock, or even about the dinner tray. Things were happening too fast for her. On an impulse she crossed the room to the door. No, the door was unlocked. And the dinner tray was gone.

Had Aunt Abbie taken it with her? No, she had left empty handed, unless the dinner tray, like the roses, had somehow become invisible. Perhaps the nightly visitor had only been someone coming after the tray.

Maybe, she thought, maybe I dreamed the whole thing, the dinner tray, the nightly visitor. She had pinched herself, but what did that mean? She might have dreamed that she pinched herself.

With a shake of the head she tried the only other door in the room. It led to a bathroom, complete with tub, of an antiquated variety, but a tub nonetheless, and a basin and stool.

"Well, at least I have the comforts of home," she said to herself, adding, "More or less." For that she could no doubt thank the sisters who had installed the wiring, before the house burned; or else the unidentified relative who must have rebuilt the house after the fire.

She turned a faucet and waited patiently for a few seconds. Nothing happened. In dismay, she turned the other faucet over the basin, and then the two at the tub, leaving them all open. Not one drop of water came out. The ingenious relative had not, it seemed, carried his modernization project to its completion.

She returned to the bedroom. The robe, still lying on the bed, caught her eyes and she snatched it up. For a moment she felt the impulse to rip it apart, to vent her annoyance and frustration on the delicate fabric. With forced calm she dropped it to the bed again. She was not a woman to lose her temper, or give free rein to her emotions. This was unpleasant, true, but she would remain calm. That was what she had always done, and what she would continue to do.

For the moment she would make do, and when she had her chat with Aunt Christine, she would ask about the lack of water. And later, when everything had been satisfactorily put in order, they would all laugh about these silly little inconveniences, she along with the rest, and no one would think of calling her "funny."

She removed her suit, the one she had worn the day before, from the armoire and donned it. It was crumpled and anything but fresh, but at least it was better than that silly robe they had provided her. And if she could not clean up, she at least had a comb in her purse, and some fresh lipstick. Thank God she still had her purse.

The results of her efforts, as viewed in the mirror over the dresser, were somewhat disappointing, but with a final assurance that they would suffice, she left her room and made her way down the stairs to the hall below.

Once at the bottom, however, her courage paled. She had seen nothing of the downstairs portion of the house the previous night with the exception of the hall itself and the room in which she had waited for Aunt Christine. It was a vast house, and the long rows of doors, still all closed, stretched cheerlessly down either wall. Where on earth was she to find the others? Aunt Christine had provided her no directions for finding the dining room, nor had Aunt Abbie thought of this difficulty.

She started slowly down the hall, listening for the sound of voices to tell her which room they were in. She reached the opposite end of the hall without hearing a sound. Whatever faults these people possessed, no one could accuse them of being boisterous at breakfast.

The little room she had seen before was empty. There was, she discovered, another door leading from it or she could return to the hall and start trying the other doors along its length. From outside the house had looked frighteningly large; she had the impression she could wander for days seeking its occupants.

"Now that's silly," she scolded herself. "They are here, in the dining room, and that can't be too far away from the parlor."

She decided upon the little door that led from the opposite wall of the room she was in, but it offered little encouragement. It opened to another hall, a small one, that led at first glance nowhere. A closer look told her that it had at one time gone somewhere after all, but one end of it had long since been boarded up, liter-ally chopped off by the addition of a makeshift wall. With mounting regrets she tried one of the two doors offered by the remaining section of the little hall.

Another empty room presented itself, this one a study or a den of some sort. It was in fact difficult to tell what purpose some of the rooms might have served. They seemed to be furnished simply for the sake of filling them up rather than serving any particular need; but then, with so many rooms, many of them would be rather superfluous, no doubt.

Another door led her into what might have been a pantry, except that there was no evidence of a kitchen nearby. No doubt it was some sort of storage room, no longer needed. All the rooms were covered with the same layer of filth that she had seen everywhere she had been so far.

The room beyond was another den, or perhaps a library, judging from the case of books on one wall. This one had any number of exits, one of which led her into—what? A bedroom? There was a bed, a metal framed affair, but the bed seemed more like an afterthought. Perhaps, she concluded, a makeshift sickroom for some member of the family who had been unable to manage the long flight of stairs to the second floor.

Room after room seemed as lacking in apparent function as the first, and each of them as empty of any occupants. She had intended to leave the doors open behind her, but the first two had swung stubbornly shut and she had given up the attempt. Now, as she tried to retrace her steps, she found herself in still more rooms; different ones, she thought, from the ones she had already seen. Or were they? It was impossible to say. The furnishings were not much different from one room to the next.

Of course if she reentered the room with the bed or the little pantry-storage room, she would have recognized them, but despite the certainty that she was following the same route she had taken, she saw neither of these two rooms. She came into room after empty room, and there were doors, more doors than she would have thought possible in any single house.

With sudden panic, she realized that she was lost. For a moment she felt an impulse to run from door to door.

"This is ridiculous," she told herself firmly, fighting back that urge to hysteria. "No matter how big this house is, these rooms can't go on forever."

The statement was lacking conviction. If ever a house could go on forever, she was ruefully afraid that Kelsey House would be the one. It wasn't a house at all, it was a maze, a web of useless rooms and closed doors; and it was laughing at her. The house itself was watching her, laughing at her confusion and fright. She could feel it. At any moment she expected it to say, "Jenny, Jenny, eat a daisy, Jenny, Jenny, you are crazy."

"Stop it," she ordered herself. "You're allowing your imagination to run away with you, Jennifer."

But it was there still, that feeling of being watched. She looked around again, but the room was still empty. Only instinct, some certainty that came from within, hinted that she was not alone. There was an eerie moment of conviction, when the presence that she felt was not physical at all, but had only intruded itself upon her mind. She shook her head firmly.

"The windows," she said in a rising voice. The rooms all had windows, and from them she could see where she was. With a new burst of hope she ran to the window nearest her and peered out. A tree—what was it, a pear tree?—old and gnarled, hovered near the glass, all but blocking the view. There were bushes beyond it, and more trees. She had only seen the front of the house from outside, in the dark, and at the time she had been more observant of the scene on the lawn, that peculiar dancing that was going on, than she had been of the grounds. The growth outside gave her no clue to her location in the house, except that she was not at the front. She was sure of that.

She had been at the front when she started out, though; she had followed the hall back to the front of the house, and had started from there. When had she turned? She tried to think back over the rooms she had come through, but they ran together in her mind. And the house was not straight, there was that funny angle to the wings.

She wanted to cry with frustration. She had the same odd sensation of unreality that she had had last night in the woods, a sense of being apart from time and the world, in another dimension as it were.

And then—had her senses been affected by all that had happened, or was that a breeze? Not just a breeze, more like a cold chill. She turned, startled, her eyes darting frantically about the room. The door across the room—was it the one through which she had entered— was swinging shut, closing itself. She stood frozen, watching it until it had slammed shut with a loud crash that echoed through the house, hurrying from room to room just as she had done. She thought, why I'm like an echo. I'm no more real than that sound. I've never been real. I've never been more than an echo of life, of reality.

That door had been closed before, she was sure of it. All of the doors had been closed, all the way through the crazy house. Why should this one be an exception?

She moved slowly across the room, stubbornly fighting down an urge to run, to scream, to do something other than remain calm. It took her a full moment to cross the room, and that long again to summon the courage to reach for the knob.

The door was locked. No, that wasn't possible. The locks were the old fashioned sort that would require a key to operate, to lock or unlock. There were no night latches here at Kelsey House. The door could not have been locked without a key, and there was no key in evidence. Unless the key were on the opposite side, in which case she had only to stoop and put her eye to the keyhole, and she would see it. But she remained standing.

She tried the knob again. The knob turned, just as a knob should do; but the door remained locked.

"It's stuck," she told herself. "It isn't locked at all, it's only stuck. Doors do that. When it's wet, the frames warp, and the door jams shut."

Of course, it wasn't wet at all, but dry and dusty in the house.

"A good tug will open it. All I have to do is hold the knob firmly and yank the door toward me."

She brought her hand back from the knob. She held her breath, listening. She was imagining things, she must be. It sounded as if there were someone breathing on the other side of the door—but it couldn't be, no matter how much it sounded like it.

There was a perfectly logical explanation. There was probably a window open in the next room, and the wind was blowing the curtains, and the curtains were those wispy affairs that sounded, when they rustled in the breeze, like someone breathing. It was the same breeze that had blown the door open, and then shut again, and now the door was merely stuck. And she was being overemotional and not a little bit silly.

Except, there was no breeze stirring.

CHAPTER SIX

"Oh, there you are."

Jennifer jumped at the unexpected voice. Her eyes wide, she turned, expecting to see the devil himself standing behind her. It was only Aunt Christine, smiling brightly at her.

"I couldn't find the dining room," Jennifer explained lamely. She knew that it sounded foolish, but what was she to say: that she had been lost in this silly old house; that she had been frightened out of her wits by a little breeze? That she had thought she heard someone breathing?

"Why you were practically there," Aunt Christine told her with a small chuckle, although Jennifer saw little humor in the situation. "But then this house is large and not too well laid out, I'll admit. You really shouldn't wander about like this until you're more accustomed to it."

And there, through the next door, was the main hall, and Jennifer hadn't gone very far at all. Three or four rooms, she would have thought by the distance. But she had taken a wrong turn somewhere and had gone off down a wing of the house, circling about. If she had kept on, she would have found her way back in another moment or two.

They crossed the hall, entering a door on the opposite side and almost to the end, and they were in the dining room. There were a number of people in the room. At a glance Jennifer saw that all of them wore the same robes as Aunt Christine and Aunt Abbie, with one exception. There was an old gentleman seated near the end of the table, and he wore ordinary-looking trousers and shirt.

With a flush of embarrassment, Jennifer realized that the family were members of a cult of some sort. There were cults of all sorts, she knew from the Sunday supplements: nudists, for one, but there were others too, religious and all. Aunt Christine and the others were merely part of a cult that required the women to dress in this peculiar fashion.

"This is Jennifer Rand, Elenora's daughter," Aunt Christine was saying, laying a hand upon Jennifer's shoulder. To Jennifer she said, "You know Abbie, of course. Next to her is Irene, your mother's sister, and Marge, and Helen. And that is Marcella over there."

Jennifer gave each of them a smile and a murmured "How do you do." The names meant nothing to her; she had thought perhaps one of them would recall some memory, some mention by her mother that had heretofore eluded her. But they were all new to her. She tried to commit each name to memory.

"We had hoped Lydia would be with us, but she was delayed. She'll join us soon, I'm sure," Aunt Christine said, finishing the introductions.

Lydia. Aunt Lydia. It was the first name that meant anything to Jennifer; but what? There was a familiar ring, but whatever it was that almost popped to the surface of her mind disappeared again. No doubt she had heard her mother mention the name at some time or another.

"And that is your mother's seat," Aunt Christine said finally, indicating the first of two empty chairs before them. "Right next to yours, dear."

It was another peculiar habit, not to say a morbid one, saving an empty seat for a member of the family who has passed away. But then, the family was a strange one. Nothing seemed impossible for them.

Her first thought as she seated herself was that Aunt Christine had neglected to introduce the old gentleman seated at the end of the table beside her. Nor had he expected it apparently, because he had not looked up during the introductions. His frail old shoulders were bent over the table, his dull eyes stared absentmindedly at the plate before him. He was unbelievably old, she realized, a faded shell of a man, scarcely aware of anything about him.

She realized now that he was the only male at the table. The others seated with her were all women. In fact, except for the hired man who had found her on the road and led her to the house, this was the only man she had seen since her arrival.

"Is the whole family here?" she asked on an impulse, directing the question to Aunt Christine.

"No, I'm afraid not," Aunt Christine answered, seating herself at the opposite end, at the head of the table. "Most of those who went naturally never returned, unless they simply wanted to be here with us, like—like one or two have done over the years."

Naturally they never returned, Jennifer repeated the phrase silently to herself. And I can't say I blame them, I don't think I shall either, when I have gone. Which, she amended quickly, will be soon. She turned toward the old gentleman.

"I'm afraid I missed your name," she addressed him, little caring whether anyone caught the inference.

"Oh, that's Morgan, Mr. Kelsey," Aunt Christine answered for him. "My husband."

Jennifer remembered then, with a start, her meeting on the road the night before, and the hired man's comment. She laughed aloud.

"Mr. Kelsey. Well, I'm glad to see you." She continued to address her remarks to him, although he made no response to her attention but only stared silently down at the table before him. "I didn't expect to see you, I'm afraid. Your man, the one who brought me up from the road last night, told me you had been done in."

She looked significantly up the table toward her Aunt Christine. "He said Mrs. Kelsey had done him in a long time ago."

Aunt Christine seemed unperturbed by the remark. She laughed and said, "Oh, Wilfred has never forgiven me." Mr. Kelsey still said nothing.

Jennifer found herself wondering whether Wilfred

was the hired man, or someone she hadn't yet encountered. And what hadn't he forgiven her anyway? The difficulty in talking with these people is that you were never sure whether their remarks were intended as answers to your questions or not.

The others had followed this conversation silently and with polite attention. Now, at the sound of a footstep in the hall, they all looked in that direction. There was a sudden air of expectancy about the table, and Jennifer, sensing it, turned with them to look toward the door from the hall.

There was a lengthy silence and then another footstep, further away. Whoever was there had, it seemed, decided not to come in, and with the moving on of that presence, something in the atmosphere seemed to relax subtly.

Jennifer glanced toward her aunt. "We have another guest," Aunt Christine said. "You'll meet her in due time." She looked pointedly toward her plate.

As the night before, on her tray, the dinnerware was again spotlessly clean, Jennifer noticed; although, she realized unhappily, the chair she was sitting in was not. She ran a finger over a corner of the seat and the finger came away black with dust. She would indeed be happy when she could get in her car and leave.

"My car," she said aloud, suddenly remembering where it was. "It was stuck down the road. I ran it into a creek. I wonder if your man couldn't bring it around for me, if he hasn't already done so?"

Again she had addressed her remarks to Mr. Kelsey,

and again it was Aunt Christine who answered.

"Your car? I don't really think you'll have much need for that. The grounds are large, but there's really no place to drive. Most of the land is wooded and has never been cleared, don't you see."

"But I will need it," Jennifer argued, although she was careful to avoid sounding difficult, as her mother had used to put it. She added hopefully, "My clothes are in it. All my luggage. I left everything in the trunk."

"Oh dear," Aunt Christine said, appearing concerned for the first time. "Didn't Abbie bring you a gown? I gave her specific instructions to bring one to your room first thing this morning."

Jennifer very nearly expressed her real opinion of the costume that had been provided for her, but she restrained herself. She knew from experience that too determined an attitude only created greater resistance. And she did not want to offend any of these people, however odd she thought them, if only because she needed help. She could not leave if she could not get her car out of that stream, and she could not do that without help, which she certainly would not get by angering them.

So she said, lamely, "It didn't fit."

Aunt Christine appeared quite relieved to learn that the difficulty was such a minor one. "Well, that's no problem. I'll have another sent up for you right after breakfast. Abbie will bring it to your room, won't you, Abbie?"

"Oh, I'd be delighted," Abbie said enthusiastically.

She looked around the table, and the other women, who had remained silent, all smiled faintly and nodded their approval of this solution to the problem.

"My room," Jennifer said, reminded now of the nightly incident and her mysterious visitor. "Aunt Christine, there was someone in my room last night."

"How very nice. But I do hope, dear, that you will bear in mind, most of us retire fairly early here."

"But it wasn't...."

"Do you say grace?"

Jennifer caught her breath at the interruption. Now this was maddening. How could she get the first degree of sense out of them if they did not allow her to pursue a single subject to its conclusion? She started to object, but she saw that the others at the table were still staring at her, waiting with what seemed impatience for her to permit the start of breakfast. And she herself, she realized suddenly, was starving. The last thing she had eaten had been a cold sandwich at some little shop along the way, and that had been at lunchtime yesterday.

"You naughty girl," Aunt Abbie addressed her in a loud stage whisper, leaning across the table to wag a finger at her. "You didn't touch your dinner last night."

"Oh." Jennifer slammed her hand angrily down upon the surface of the table. That was pouring salt upon some sensitive wounds.

"Is something the matter?" Aunt Christine asked from her place at the head of the table.

Jennifer looked about the table at the faces turned expectantly toward her. Yes, she had seen those looks before. Her guess had been correct, she was sure of it. They were all of them waiting for her to protest about the food, or rather the lack of food, and that would give them all a good laugh—at her expense. She had been through this sort of thing so often. She had thought it was all behind her, but it seemed it was not.

"Yes," she said, seizing upon the first thought that came to mind. "There's no water in my room."

"Water?" Aunt Christine repeated the word as though Jennifer might have used a foreign phrase. "Water. I'm afraid I never even thought of that. But I'll see that it's looked into. Grace?"

Her face flushing angrily, Jennifer bowed her head and mumbled a blessing, which she amended slightly to cover her current situation: "...guide over me and bless me, and help me to get my car out of the creek."

When she looked up she discovered that no one, not one of the others, had bowed their heads. They were sitting just as before, staring at her as though she were some sort of freak. Then, as if on signal, they all looked away.

"They are mad," she told herself silently, her eyes slowly circling the table. "They are every one of them as mad as hatters, and I must leave this house right after breakfast."

But, she reminded herself, there was a problem. Her car was still stuck in the mud somewhere; to tell the truth, she did not have the vaguest idea where it was even. Which way had they come through those awful woods last night, and how far? If only that man hadn't walked so fast, she might have had some idea of the path they had taken, might have been able to watch for landmarks.

Well, he could just walk right back and get her car out of that creek for her before the day was out, she would insist upon that. She would find him herself and tell him so, and go along to see that he did it. She had seen as much as she wished to see of Kelsey House and its occupants, and she did not much care if they were family.

The girl at her left, beyond the empty seat that had been saved for her mother, was handing her something in a bowl. With a curt smile, Jennifer took the bowl and looked down into it.

It was empty. Not one crumb, not even a stain to indicate that it might have, say when it had started at the other end of the table, held anything.

She looked up, startled. They were passing platters and bowls and trays and helping themselves generously. It might have been a truly bountiful breakfast, but for one detail. The dishes were empty. There was not a trace of food anywhere on the table that she could see.

And the worst of it was, they were eating. Across from Jennifer, Aunt Abbie held a spoon in one hand and dipped it daintily toward her plate. She carried the spoonful of air to her mouth, and chewed at it

This, Jennifer thought, was carrying a joke too far. Fun, if one could call it that, was fun, but she could very well faint away from hunger while they carried on their tasteless joke.

I will not give in, she swore stubbornly, fighting down the angry words that had risen in her throat. She had that, certainly, a stubborn streak that even her mother had not been able to break. Quiet and meek she might be, but she could be as stubborn as a mule when the occasion demanded; and she thought that it did now.

I will sit here just as long as they do, she vowed silently, and I will pretend that I have not even noticed their little game. And when they finally do serve breakfast, I may even tell them that I am stuffed and cannot eat another bite.

But they did not serve any food. They kept right on with the pantomime of eating what they had already, or rather, what they did not have. All of them pretended to eat, that is, except Jennifer and one other member of the group.

With a sense of genuine relief, Jennifer stole a glance at the young girl beside her on her left. She was scarcely more than a child, pretty in a china doll fashion; her skin incredibly white, like fine marble, and her hair a blue black cloud that framed a face of almost heartbreaking sweetness. And, most endearing of all from Jennifer's point of view, she was the only one at the table, except for Jennifer herself, who was not taking part in the joke. She sat without touching her utensils, staring idly down at her empty plate.

"The poor child is probably starving," Jennifer thought; then she did something quite impulsive and most unusual for her. She reached over and gently placed her hand upon one of the girl's hands.

The girl jumped, startled, and turned to look at her. Jennifer winked—a quick wink, just enough to let the child know that she understood what was going on, and that she appreciated the girl's refusal to take part in it. They exchanged quick, conspiratorial smiles.

"You're not eating," Aunt Christine said unexpectedly, interrupting their silent exchange.

"We're not hungry," Jennifer answered calmly for both of them. There, she thought, score one up for her. Now they knew that she didn't care that much for their silly game.

"In fact," she added on an impulse, "I wonder if you would just excuse me."

She pushed her chair back, noting the dust with disgust, and rose quickly without waiting for anyone to excuse her. Whatever their purpose was, she had suffered quite enough of it for one morning. If neither Aunt Christine nor her husband would see that she got her car back, she would look after it herself. After all, so far as she knew upon reflection, the car was not really stuck in the mud. It had simply stalled on her after the unexpected dunking. There was every likelihood that it would start by this time, now that it had dried out.

If that were the case, she could quite easily just drive away, without help from anyone. She had made up her mind that she did not care to spend another night in Kelsey House. She did not like it any more than she liked her new found relatives.

She went into the hall and started toward the stairs to go up. But she stopped at the foot of the stairs. She had a glimpse of a woman on the landing, disappearing out of sight around the turn there.

"There's no getting away from them," Jennifer thought with annoyance. She placed her foot on the first step and stopped again. She had left the occupants of Kelsey House at breakfast; no one had left the table before her. So who was this she had just glimpsed, mounting the stairs before her? The white robe was no help; they all dressed alike, and she had not seen the face, only the long, dark hair flowing down the back. But it could not be any of those she had already met.

She remembered then the footstep outside the dining room door, that had come and gone, and Aunt Christine's explanation that there was another person in the house whom she had not yet met.

It occurred to her at once that here was someone who had taken no part in the cruel joke the others were playing at her expense. Here, perhaps, was an ally, someone who could help her find her way back to her car.

"Wait," she called aloud, but above she heard a rustling that faded into the distance as the woman went on.

The long dark hair; she had a sudden vision of the mysterious visitor in her room last night. She had not seen the visitor's face, but she had seen the long dark hair flowing over her robe. She had noticed it and remembered it because it was so like her mother's hair had been, although ordinarily her mother had worn hers up. But at night it had been down, dark and flowing, its color and lustre refusing to fade despite advancing years.

She had found her intruder. Whoever the woman was who had just disappeared up the stairs, this unnamed house guest, she was the same who had so boldly made her way into the bedroom the night before. Why, Jennifer wondered?

Her heart pounding, Jennifer raced up the stairs, rounding the turn at the landing. She wanted to meet this other woman, wanted to see her face to face, and enlist her aid if she could.

She hurried to the top of the stairs, in time to catch only another glimpse of the stranger, at the far end of the hall, going through a door.

"Oh wait, please," she called impatiently, but the woman was gone. Jennifer quickly went along the length of the hall, frightened without quite knowing why, but eager to catch up to the mysterious stranger.

All of the doors were closed but one, and beyond that door was another stairway, not like the sweeping graceful stairs that led from the main hall downstairs to the second floor, but a narrow spiraling tunnel that led sharply upward. Jennifer remembered the turret, the little tower that rose over the rest of Kelsey House. These stairs undoubtedly went up to the turret

The stairs lay in shadows, and she saw nothing, but just as she paused at the bottom, a door above creaked noisily on its hinges. This was the door, then, through which the woman had gone.

"Well, she can't go any farther," Jennifer told herself, starting up. She reached the top, and she was in a small, round room; and it was empty.

Before her another door stood open, and through it she could see the blue of the sky outside. She crossed the room and looked out. A narrow wooden walkway circled about the turret and beyond its rusted railings was the lawn at the front of Kelsey House, sweeping smoothly down toward the woods, and in the distance were the woods themselves, brilliant already with autumn colors.

A flash of white just out of the range of her vision caught her eye. She looked off to the side. There was no one to be seen, but she was sure the woman was there, hidden from her sight by the curve of the turret.

Of all the silly things, Jennifer thought, stepping out onto the walkway. Why is she running and hiding herself like this? I'm no threat to anyone.

The wood creaked and sagged beneath her feet, and she took hold of the narrow rail that provided the only barrier between her and the fall to the ground far below. She started slowly forward, the sharp curve of the structure hiding from her any clue of what lay ahead. There was nothing but the little space in which she moved, one cautious step at a time.

She paused once, looking down, and was surprised to see the family below. They were all there, so far as she could tell at a glance, on the distant lawn, staring up at her. Unmoving, they watched her move.

But how on earth had they known she was up here? Why had they left their "breakfast" to come to the lawn and observe her? And why were they watching her in that intent fashion?

Her eyes on them, fascinated and puzzled by their appearance, she inched slowly forward, continuing around the turret. Their gazes followed her.

Suddenly the walkway was gone. She brought her foot down to find nothing but air beneath it.

CHAPTER SEVEN

With a little scream she fell against the wall, clinging to it, her heart in her throat. She had not yet brought her weight down upon that foot; had she done so, she would certainly have fallen to her death. There, just in front of her, the platform on which she had been walking suddenly ended. The wood had rotted and fallen away long ago. Another step, and she would have walked over its edge, falling to the ground before the very eyes of the people watching below.

Trembling, she inched her way backward, afraid to turn about until she felt the framing of the doorway behind her, and she was through it, back safely into the little round turret room. Her breath came in rapid, uneven gasps, and her heart still pounded at a frantic pace.

I might have been killed, she told herself, trembling anew as the thought came to her. I could have fallen and broken my neck. And no one had tried to stop her or warn her; not one person had raised a hand to save her life. They had all stood on the lawn far below and watched her make her way forward, knowing what lay before her, and knowing that she would surely fall.

In those few moments Jennifer's fright at what had nearly happened to her had erased any other considerations from her mind. As the first shock waves receded, she thought of something else. The woman, the stranger she had been following; what had happened to her?

She had not fallen; there was no sign of a body sprawled upon the lawn, as there certainly would be. And she could not have gone on around the turret, without walking on air.

Or had she even been out there? Jennifer wondered. Had she even been in the turret? The dust here looked undisturbed, as if no one had been here in years. Indeed, all of the house looked the same way.

Had Jennifer deceived herself into thinking the woman had come this way, tricked into that belief by an open door below, and a creaking one above?

She looked about again. There was no other way out of this room save for the little walkway outside. The woman could not have been here at all. She had gone through another door of the many along the hall, and left the entrance to the stairs open as a decoy.

Jennifer made her way down the spiraling stairs to the floor below, and carefully closed the door after herself, lest someone else make the same mistake she had. Aunt Christine was just hurrying along the hallway toward her.

"The turret is rather dangerous," Aunt Christine greeted her as she approached. "We never use it these days."

Jennifer looked at her for a moment without replying.

Then, still saying nothing, she went by her and let herself into her own room, and locked the door.

She had nearly been killed, and no one had cared. Indeed, if anything, they had seemed quite fascinated by the show, as it seemed to be for them.

For the second time, Jennifer realized that she might be in danger here, surrounded by a houseful of madness.

"I must get away from here," she told herself, and immediately asked, "But how?"

* * * * * *

"Jennifer, it's time for lunch," Aunt Christine called from the hall,

Jennifer remained stubbornly silent, her eyes on the door. After a time she saw the knob turn as Aunt Christine tried the door and found it locked.

"Jennifer," Aunt Christine called again.

This is silly, Jennifer told herself. I'm not hurting anyone but myself by sitting here and pouting. She half rose to answer the door, then seated herself again on the bed. No, it would do them good to worry about her. Maybe they wouldn't think their little game was so funny if they thought she really was going to starve, and they might have a corpse on their hands.

After a little while she heard Aunt Christine moving away down the hall. Jennifer opened her purse and again removed the letter that she had originally received from Aunt Christine. She had been studying it most of the morning already.

Take Bellen Road off Peters Road...but that still didn't tell her anything about where she was. She had been driving north, and then west—no, east, because the sun had been behind her when it set. And then she had gone right; or had it been left?

It was impossible. Her mind seemed to be refusing to function as it should. She seemed at moments to be no longer in possession of her faculties, as though someone else had taken control of her reasoning processes. It was like being someplace that you knew, but in a thick fog, so that even familiar objects took on a strange appearance and nothing seemed quite what it should be.

She put a hand to her forehead. The strain was beginning to tell on her, that was all it was. If she had something to eat....

She sat upright, dropping the letter from her hands. The doorknob had turned again. Someone was trying the door.

"Aunt Christine?" she called aloud. The knob stopped turning, but there was no answer. Someone outside in the hall had tried the door and found it locked.

"Aunt Christine?" she called again. Still only silence came back to her.

More puzzled than frightened, she stood and crossed the room to the door, listening. No sounds; nothing to tell her if her visitor had gone or was waiting on the other side of the door; waiting...for what?

Again the knob turned slowly, noisily. Jennifer found herself staring at it as though hypnotized by its circling motion. She knew the door was locked and yet she found herself waiting for it to open, to swing on its hinges and reveal the intruder to her.

"Who's there?" she called aloud, forcing herself from her immobility. She would not stand there like a frightened ninny and let just anyone intrude upon her privacy. Someone must give her an explanation, or she would go mad.

She turned the key, despite trembling fingers, unlocking the door. For a moment she hesitated. Then, seizing the knob herself, she threw the door open—to find herself facing an empty hall.

There was no one there. She stepped out into the hall, peering in both directions. But the hall was truly empty.

It was quite simple, she told herself. Whoever was out here had heard her turn the key in the lock, and had gone into one of the other rooms, behind one of those stupid doors along the hall. Again she looked in both directions, looking for some indication of which room had given refuge. But the doors were all closed, all of them. Nothing was amiss.

She started in the direction of the stairs. Mad or not mad, Aunt Christine simply must provide an explanation for the goings on around this house.

"My nerves just can't endure any more of this," she told herself.

Behind her, a door closed. She whirled about, staring down the long hall.

Which door had closed? And why? All of the doors

had been closed already when she had come out into the hall. Nothing had been open except...except her own door.

Her door was closed now. She had left it open when she came into the hall, and she had not closed it when she started for the stairs. It had been wide ajar.

It was closed now, just like all the others. She walked slowly back toward her room, coming to a stop outside her door.

Someone was in her room, someone who waited for her to enter—to do whatever it was they had come to do. She thought of the turret, and the near accident there. Had that been deliberate, and not an accident? Did someone really mean to do her harm, to take...she hesitated even to think this...to take her life?

What could she do? Certainly it was pointless for her to go downstairs for help. Whatever was happening in the house, they were all a part of it. She was, in the truest sense of the word, alone.

And perhaps she was imagining all this. She was very jumpy, her nerves were raw, and her imagination was running away with itself. All of the doors in the house close themselves if left open. It is something to do, no doubt with the way the house was built

She turned the knob, pushed, and the door swung lazily open. The room was empty; no one waited to seize her and do horrible things to her. A cool breeze brushed her face, making obvious what must have happened; the breeze from the open window had blown the door shut. It was as simple as that.

"What a baby I am," she chided herself, closing the door and reentering the room. She sat down on the bed and for a moment laughed silently at her own jumpy nerves.

But the breeze had not turned the knob of her door when she had been inside here, she thought her laughter fading. No, someone had been in the hall earlier and had tried to enter her room. And the breeze....

The breeze! She jumped from the bed and stared at the window. The window had been closed, impossible for her to open. It had been closed a moment before when she had left the room and gone into the hall; and now it was open.

She went to the window, staring out. The lawn was two stories below, with no means of descent from here other than the obvious one of falling. Nor was there any walkway or balcony or ledge outside. No, no one had left the room by this exit. Nor could they have left by the hall door without going by her.

"I am imagining things," she told herself, speaking very slowly and distinctly. "So much has happened that I am no longer thinking clearly."

That at least was the truth. She was no longer thinking clearly. Was it the tension, the strangeness of the situation in which she found herself; perhaps the lack of food?

Something was happening to her. She felt light headed and not at all herself. Was this how one felt when one had been drinking? It seemed to match the description; but her experience was limited to a few glasses of wine, so she could not really know.

Again she had the feeling of being apart from herself and from life, as if she were in a dream. None of this seemed quite real, or as if it could really be happening to her.

"I may be losing my mind," she thought. That would explain everything.

Forcefully she pushed that thought aside. If she once allowed herself to begin contemplating that, she knew the idea would grow and grow in her mind, until she accepted it as the truth.

There was an explanation for everything. "I must have opened that window myself, and I've simply forgotten about it."

"But when?" The question came unbidden into her mind. "When did I open it?"

CHAPTER EIGHT

By the time Aunt Christine arrived to announce dinner, Jennifer was ready to admit defeat. Pride or no pride, she was literally starving to death. Certainly, she assured herself as she came downstairs, they had finished with their preposterous joke and were ready to begin treating her as a guest should be treated. They must see the harm they were doing.

"Oh, there you are," Aunt Christine greeted her as she entered the dining room. This time Jennifer had come along the hall to the right doorway, and had found the dining room without incident.

"We had begun to worry about you," Aunt Abbie said.

"I should think you would, you nasty old women," Jennifer thought; "I have been starved almost to death, nearly killed in a fall, and all but assaulted in my own room."

Aloud, she said, "Thank you, I'm afraid I haven't been very good company."

"Helen prepared this dinner especially for you, because you seemed to be unhappy this morning," Aunt Christine explained. "I hope you like it."

"I'm certain I shall," Jennifer said. She was prepared to like virtually anything that was set before her. She could not remember when she had ever been so hungry. She seated herself quickly, ignoring the empty chair beside her, saved for her mother. She nodded to the others about the table. Aunt Abbie leaned toward her.

"Didn't your new robe fit either?" she asked, indicating the gray suit Jennifer still wore.

"I'm afraid not," Jennifer said coldly. That was one point she refused to give in on; but she did not want to provoke a quarrel, not before she had eaten. Later, when she had some food in her, she would clear things up.

"Oh dear," Aunt Abbie replied, shaking her head sadly. "Then I don't see how you can take part in the rites."

"The rites?" For a moment Jennifer did not understand. Then it came back to her, that odd dancing on the lawn that she had witnessed on her arrival. Aunt Abbie had called them the rites. "Oh, yes, the rites," she said lamely.

"Of course, if Christine thinks it will be all right," Abbie offered, glancing questioningly toward Aunt Christine at the head of the table.

"Now Abbie," Aunt Christine said, wagging a finger at her. "You know the rules as well as I do. We shall simply have to find another robe for Jennifer."

"But she'll miss the rites," Abbie argued. She turned back to Jennifer. "They're right after dinner, you know. There simply wouldn't be time to find a robe for you before they began."

"I think," Jennifer interrupted the family disagreement, "that perhaps the best solution all around would be to give me my own clothing. If someone would just lead me back to my car, where my luggage is still waiting...."

"Oh, that would never do," Abbie said, her voice rising to a shocked level. "We will have to find a robe for you, that's all there is to that. No, I'm afraid your own clothes would never do for the rites. Everyone must wear a robe. It's always been like that."

Jennifer sighed aloud. Now how had she gotten herself involved in all this nonsense over the rites, in which she was not at all interested?

"I think we may start dinner now," Aunt Christine suggested, handing a platter to the woman at her left.

Jennifer was not at all surprised to discover that again the platters and bowls were all empty. They were not yet ready to end their fun. They had probably already eaten their dinner, sometime before she was called, and they were now going through the same elaborate pantomime as at breakfast, pretending to eat from empty dishes.

Marcella had handed Jennifer an empty bowl. Jennifer let it slip through her fingers. It fell to the table with a crash, breaking into several pieces. There was a stunned silence about the table; all eyes were upon her. At any minute she expected them to begin laughing.

"I must have food," she said aloud. "I demand that you give me something to eat."

There was a long pause. Jennifer was prepared to stand her ground now. She had never before had to stand up for herself, but necessity gave her the strength to do so now.

Aunt Christine got swiftly up from her seat. "Why certainly, dear," she said. "I'm so happy that you're hungry again."

For a moment Jennifer felt relief. They were going to give in after all, without the necessity of a fight. All it had taken were a few firmly spoken words.

Aunt Christine came hurriedly along the table, to where Jennifer sat. She reached past Jennifer, seizing a large, empty platter.

"Here," she said, deftly spooning out whatever was supposed to be on the platter onto Jennifer's plate. "I think you'll like this, dear, Helen fixed it especially for you."

Jennifer opened her mouth to speak, anger rising within her. But the words did not come. She was gripped by a sense of frustration, of hopelessness. It was no use, they would not give her the food she wanted. She could feel reason slipping even further from her, and a sense of helpless panic came over her.

Wordlessly she stood and started from the room. Perhaps she thought dizzily, it is I who am mad. Perhaps there really is food on the table and the chairs are not ruining my skirt with filth.

"Jennifer?" Aunt Christine called after her.

Without looking back, Jennifer left the room and ran to her own bedroom. She threw herself across her bed. Impossible though it seemed, she was the victim of some monstrous scheme concocted among them for purposes she could not fathom.

"I will not beg," she promised herself. "I will sit in my room until they promise to give up this nonsense and serve me some real food."

"If I haven't died in the meantime of starvation," she added. She truly did not feel well. She was weak and frightfully tired. That was the lack of food, undoubtedly, and her nerves too. Her tranquilizers were in a case in her luggage, where they were doing not the slightest good.

She lay for a moment staring at the ceiling. They were all mad? Or—and this was a chilling alternative—or she was. It was difficult to believe that this was only a joke. The entire family seemed so earnest in their belief that there was food on the table. They saw it, and she did not. Either they were crazy, or she was.

How did one tell?

She closed her eyes, feeling fatigue washing over her like the waves of the sea. She knew one thing. She had had no delusions before she came here. And there was no mistake about the fact that they were trying to keep her from leaving. Every mention of her car and her clothing was shrugged off.

They could not keep her a prisoner here, though. She would leave. "In the morning," she promised herself as she drifted off to sleep, "I will leave on my own. I will start through those woods and I will not stop until I have found the road again, and my car."

* * * * * * *

The cold air from the window was blowing over her, chilling her although she still wore her suit. She sat up, intending to close the window. She paused, listening; shook her head and listened again. No, it wasn't just the wind, and she hadn't dreamed it. Someone had called her name.

"Who's there?" she called into the darkness. Why hadn't she remembered to turn on the light before she fell asleep? My God, she thought, I didn't even lock the door.

As if in answer to her thoughts, someone tapped at the door, a steady, monotonous tapping sound that grew steadily in volume.

"Who is it?" she asked, frightened now. The door was unlocked. If whoever was there tried the door, he would find it open. The tapping continued, growing to a loud knocking that rattled the mirror over the dresser.

"Go away," Jennifer called aloud. Still the knocking continued, louder and louder until the whole room reverberated with it.

"I'm dreaming this," she told herself, clenching her hands into tight fists, and biting into her lip. She felt as if she wanted to scream, to run—only there was no place to run.

"Please, go away," she shouted, her voice almost lost in the din of the pounding.

Suddenly the knocking stopped, and the room was

silent again.

After a long time, during which no sound disturbed the silence, Jennifer rose from her bed and crossed the room slowly, expecting the door to spring open at any minute. But it remained closed, and at last she had reached it and turned the key, locking it. She hadn't the nerve to open it and see who or what might be outside. She did not care, if only they did not try to come in.

She turned the light on and went back to bed, but she was too frightened to sleep. She sat at the head of the bed, huddled into a little ball, and waited for something more to happen.

Nothing did happen, though, and finally it was morning. She had sat up most of the night, and now the window grew light with the coming of dawn, and in the distance she could make out the gray green of the trees in the woods. The night was ended.

"I can't go on like this," she told herself. Her head was throbbing. She had had no food and little sleep. She was no longer certain how much of this was actually happening to her and how much she had simply imagined; or had she simply imagined it all? Perhaps after all she would awaken soon to find herself safely at home, in her own little bed, in her nightgown, suffering from some thoughtless bedtime snack.

No, the morning was real, and this dismal room with the dirty furniture and the faded wallpaper was real. She was at Kelsey House, and she was afraid; afraid of things that she could not understand, things that she seemed helpless to do anything about.

"But I will do something about them," she said firmly, getting up from the bed. "I am leaving here today, this morning."

CHAPTER NINE

This time she did not even bother with the silly charade of breakfast. She did not know what it all meant, but she was certain that they had no intention of feeding her at these "meals."

When Aunt Christine came to tap on her door and tell her breakfast was ready, Jennifer called brightly, "I'll be right down."

She waited until she was sure her aunt had gone. Then she let herself out of her room, and took the stairs down to the first floor. In a moment she was outside, on the front porch of Kelsey House.

If the floor plan of Kelsey House was a puzzlement, however, the grounds were no less peculiar. From the diminutive porch one could look out over the sweeping lawn that Jennifer had already seen. Beyond the lawn she could see the woods thick and ominous even from this distance; they formed a solid wall, without a break in them.

And that, she told herself, was peculiar. Never mind the little path that man had led her along, hardly a path even. That, she assumed, had been some shortcut of his own.

But there would have to be a driveway, or at the very least, some sort of walkway, that led to the road. Even if the people here seldom left the house, there was the question of supplies. Notwithstanding the silly business of serving her empty dishes, they themselves had to eat some time or another. Even if they grew their own food on the grounds somewhere—and that was a possibility she might want to explore—there must certainly be other things that they would have to bring from town.

Upon reflection though she could not think of a single thing, try though she might. Nothing in the house was new. Aside from food, what exactly would they need from the outside? Clothes? That was not likely. The simple robes they wore could have been made from anything, curtains even, or fabric purchased in quantity years before. Obviously they did not use cleaning supplies, judging from the condition of the house. What else was there? Perhaps on thinking about it, the occupants of Kelsey House did not really need to make use of the nearby town. It was not a very encouraging conclusion, from her point of view.

At least, however, there was a path; a footpath, to be specific, and although it did not appear to offer any immediate means of reaching the road that lay somewhere beyond the woods, it did lead from the stairs of the porch along the width of the house, disappearing around a corner. Presumably it had to go somewhere; most paths did. On the other hand, Jennifer reminded herself, Kelsey was not like most places she had known.

She decided she would try following the path. It might very well lead her to a garden where the family grew their food; if they did not bring it in, they must raise it here themselves.

She went along the front of the house, the grass beneath her feet still damp with the morning dew. She passed the tower, its base jutting out from the house itself. Glancing upward, she shivered as she saw the dangling remnants of the walkway that encircled the structure, the walk from which she had almost fallen.

She followed the path, rounding the corner of the house, and stopped abruptly. It was like stepping suddenly into the heart of the woods. The rolling lawn, the solid foreboding facade of the house, ended at the corner, to be replaced by straggly bushes, low-hanging trees, weeds, and sagging, unpainted walls. She was reminded, as she stared at the disorder, of pictures she had seen of movie sets, with their glamorous fronts that suggested a wholeness they did not in fact possess. She was behind the set now, and the illusion was lost. But why there should be a movie set here, she had no idea.

She looked around. It had been here, somewhere on this end of the house, where she had looked out of the window when she was lost in the house. She looked about for the tree she had seen, the big one just outside the window, but there were too many of them to be certain that she had found the right one.

The thought of trees brought with it an idea that lighted a faint spark of hope within her. Some of the trees must be fruit trees. It was late in the season, no doubt, but there might be something edible on the ground. She looked about, trying to remember when apples and the like ripened, but she was not very knowledgeable about such matters.

There had been an apple tree at home when she was a girl; not that she had changed homes since then, but the tree had long since gone. It had gone the summer that her mother had discovered that she played in the tree, that the tree had become a secret place for the young Jennifer. For one whole summer Jennifer had hidden in that tree when she wanted to get away from things, to escape into a world of her own. She had climbed the tree, and played in it, and actually grown to love its gnarled, patternless branches.

One day, however, some strange men had arrived in a truck and started cutting and sawing. By the time they left there was nothing remaining of the tree but a wounded and mournful stump.

Strange, she had not thought of that tree for years. She wandered on through the thick growth, wandered because the path she had followed had ended abruptly at the corner of the house. The trees, thick overhead, shielded her from the warm beams of the morning sun, and she was reminded of the coolness of the autumn morning.

She found a tree, an apple tree, and the ground beneath it was littered with old fruit. Most of it, to be sure, was rotted or dried up, but she looked carefully about on the ground, examining each apple she found. Even the best of them was none too good—knobby, wormy looking things that made clear the fact that the tree had gone wild. But she found a handful of fruit that would be, at least in part, edible.

She bit into one of the apples eagerly, savoring the bitter, sour taste of the pulp in her mouth. She greedily devoured the few she had found, gulping down what she could of them. She began to look for more, and when she found another, her impulse was to devour it as well. She checked herself, though. If this was all she found, it might be necessary to ration them. It was impossible to say how long it would take her to find the car, and as hungry as she was now, she would certainly be even hungrier after a few hours of walking.

There was another thought too that influenced her. If there was one tree with fruit about its base, there might be others, perhaps with better offerings.

She collected all of the apples she could find that might be edible, and put them in a neat little pile at the base of the tree. She would look first to see what else she could find in the way of food to carry with her; then she would try to find her way through the woods to her car.

The brush, as she moved away from the house, had grown even thicker, and once or twice she scratched her arms on the undergrowth. Watching the ground as she was, she failed to see a low hanging branch that slapped her smartly across the face. Her hand, when she brought it away from the spot, was stained with fresh blood.

Despite what must have been another half hour

of searching, however, she found no more food. Discouraged, she decided instead to take what she had. She was tired, and before she set out she ought to get her sweater. Certainly she would need her purse, because the car keys were in it, and she had not thought to bring it out with her. There was nothing for it but to return to the house; but at least now she would have her little store of apples, so the morning was not completely wasted.

That was when she discovered that the house was no longer in sight. It should have been. She had been walking in a straight line, she thought, and the house should have been directly behind her, but it wasn't. At least, it was not visible through the trees and the brush that surrounded her.

"I am not going to let myself become terrified again," she insisted. She looked about, but nothing seemed particularly familiar. One tree looked pretty much like another, and she had failed to watch for any landmarks as she walked; her attention had been concentrated on looking for food.

Just to her right was a clump of bushes she had come through, she was certain. She held the branches apart and made her way through the growth, but instead of a small clump it proved to be a fair size patch. She found herself entangled in clinging branches and cutting thorns that added to the scratches on her arms and legs.

She was through it at last, and beyond it was a clearing; not much, but it did look familiar. If she went around that big tree...she did, without achieving anything. Her apple tree, and her little pile of apples, ought to be in sight, right in front of her there, but they were not. In fact, there was a stump there, and she didn't remember any stumps at all. And she was lost again.

She sat down on the stump, dropping her head wearily into her hands. She wanted to cry, or scream, or some such thing. She seemed unable to manage anything. It was as if Kelsey House, and even the grounds around it, deliberately set out to frustrate her efforts to leave, even her efforts to survive. They seemed to have minds of their own, minds that were set against her. Even now, lost in the woods, she did not feel alone, she felt as if she were in the presence of something that watched her and brooded, something that would not let her escape, that never meant for her to leave here.

She held her breath, listening. Was she imagining things again, or was that something moving nearby. No, this time she was definitely not imagining anything. There was somebody close at hand, someone moving about through the dense growth; someone, or something. Twigs snapped, and branches scraped against one another.

It could be someone from the house. By now they might have discovered that she had gone. She had not come down for breakfast, and undoubtedly they would have come to her room to investigate. Finding her gone, they might very well be searching for her now.

In that case, she ought to call out and tell them where she was. It was all well and good to want to be out of

Kelsey House, but being lost and alone in the woods was not any better so far as she could see.

But she did not call out just yet. What if it weren't a person at all, she asked herself, listening to the noises coming closer? What kind of animals lived in woods like these? She really did not know, but it was not hard to imagine any number of wild creatures prowling about.

The noises were closer, definitely coming in her direction. Should she run, or maybe try to climb a tree?

In the end, she did nothing but sit in fear and shiver, and watch in the direction of the crashing and crunching that moved steadily closer until the bushes parted and there in front of her was the hired man, the one who had found her on the road the night she had arrived at Kelsey.

He stopped, exactly as he had done that night, and stared at her. Whatever relief she might have felt at seeing a human being instead of some wild animal disappeared almost at once in his cold stare. It was not a pleasant look that he gave her, but one of unspeakable violence and ugliness, a look that combined dark thoughts with a bitter, just-beneath-the-surface laughter. He was amused at finding her here, she thought, amused and for some peculiar reason angry at the same time.

As for herself, Jennifer sat quietly on the stump and returned his stare for as long as she was able, which was not long at all. Her mother had always accused her of being shifty-eyed, which was not far from the truth.

She could never look anyone in the eye for long. After a moment or two, she had always done just as she did this time; she dropped her eyes to the ground. Without a word, the man started to go on.

"Wait," she called after him anxiously. Like it or not he was her only means of finding her way out of this woods. And as much as she disliked Kelsey House, even that seemed preferable to remaining lost where she was. The next noise might be a wild animal after all.

He paused and glanced back over his shoulder at her.

"I'm afraid I've lost my way," she explained, realizing that she sounded like a helpless child. "Can you lead me to where I left my car?"

He paused for a moment longer, without replying.

"Or back to Kelsey House," she suggested. She had hoped he might take her to the car, but she supposed he was part of whatever conspiracy they had formed against her. She would take her chances at Kelsey House. From there, she thought she could find the path they had taken that first night

Still without a word, he started off again. She hadn't the vaguest idea where he was leading or, if he was leading her at all. Of all the strange occupants of Kelsey, he was indeed the most flagrantly rude of the lot.

"Well," she thought, "wherever he is going, it has to be somewhere." If he was not going back to the house, perhaps after all he would lead her to the road, from which she could find her car. Or better yet, perhaps he was going to a neighboring house, where there might be ordinary people like herself, people who would help her. She jumped up from where she had been sitting and started after him, rushing to keep up with his rapid pace.

Another thought came to her as she hurried in his wake, and she called to him, asking, "Were you able to do anything about my car?" It occurred to her that for all she knew that might have been what he was attending to just now.

If he heard her question, though, he gave no evidence of it, but crashed silently onward, just as he had that other time. She knew better than to try slowing her pace, or begging him to wait. She must keep in sight of him or be lost. In directing her attention so firmly to his back, she failed again to see a low hanging branch that cracked smartly across her forehead. The sting brought tears to her eyes and she almost did come to a stubborn stop. But he was disappearing ahead of her, and she ran on to keep from losing him.

The house appeared suddenly, without warning. It was almost, she thought, as if the blasted thing were hiding itself from her, in order to watch her unseen, and then springing up when she least expected it. One minute they were surrounded by nothing but wilds, and she would have sworn there was no sight of the house before them; the next minute the house itself, grotesque and unseemly, loomed up ahead of her.

The man she was following disappeared. She turned once, looking up at the house with mixed feelings of relief and distaste, and when she looked back, her companion, if he could be called that, was gone. She could almost doubt that he had ever been there.

"Oh, do be careful," a voice said.

Jennifer jumped, startled by the unexpected sound of a voice, and turned to find herself facing Aunt Abbie. The older woman stood on the opposite side of a small bush.

"You might crush the roses," Aunt Abbie went on, indicating the bush with a protective wave of her hand over it.

It was a rose bush, Jennifer saw, or at least it looked like one, with thorns and thick stems. But there was no evidence of bloom on it, not even of buds. The flowers were as invisible as those Aunt Abbie brought to her room; as invisible as the food they served at meals in the dining room.

"I'm sorry," Jennifer stammered, pushing her matted hair back with one hand. Now why on earth, she asked herself, should I apologize for almost crushing some nonexistent flowers? Why was everything here so infuriatingly unreal? If something, anything, would only make some sense—but nothing did. At least not anymore. She was no longer able to say with certainty what was real, if any of it was, and what was imagined. And if imagined, by whom? By herself, or by them?

"You weren't in your room this morning when I brought the roses," Aunt Abbie said with a sly little grin, as if they were sharing a secret.

"No, I was walking," Jennifer told her. "I was

looking for my car."

"Your car?"

"Yes, you see...."

"Why?" Aunt Abbie seemed genuinely puzzled.

Jennifer took a deep breath, and in a patient voice, said, "It got stuck in a stream the night I arrived, and I would like to get it out. If only someone would help me find it. It's in the stream that crosses the road, I've forgotten the name...."

"Why do you want your car?" Aunt Abbie looked as if she really was trying to understand what she was being told.

Jennifer hesitated, not sure she should risk repeating that she wanted to leave. It might make them more determined to keep her here. She said, calmly, "Because all of my things are in the car, and I'm afraid they might be stolen if I don't bring them to the house."

"If you promise not to tell the others," Aunt Abbie said, leaning closer across the rose bush, "I'll do something special for you."

Jennifer's heart jumped. Aunt Abbie was offering to help her. She had understood, finally, and now she was going to show her the way to her car.

"Yes, yes, I promise to keep it from the others," she said quickly, dropping her voice instinctively to a whisper. "Please, will you help me?"

Aunt Abbie nodded. "I'll do something very special for you."

"Will you lead me to my car?"

"I'll bring you some peonies," Aunt Abbie said.

Jennifer was struck dumb. She stared in disbelief at the pleasure written on her aunt's face.

"Peonies?" she echoed finally.

"They're so lovely this year," Aunt Abbie said with enthusiasm. "I swear it, blooms the size of watermelons. But Christine doesn't like for me to bring them into the house. She doesn't like the smell of them."

"Of course," Jennifer said in weary agreement. Her hopes had faded and died. It was useless trying to get any help from them, any of them. They were all mad, and all against her. The only person who had helped her at all had been the man in the woods, and although he was rude, he had at least found her twice and led her out of the woods.

"That man," she said aloud, abandoning her previous discussion with Aunt Abbie, "the hired man. Can't he talk at all?"

"Wilfred?" Aunt Abbie was fooling with her nonexistent roses again. "He can, but he so seldom does. Not for the last twenty years. He's still angry with me, of course. He'd leave if he could."

"So would I," Jennifer thought. But she examined this new bit of information. If that man wanted to leave, perhaps she could after all make an ally of him. She would certainly give that some thought.

"Angry?" she repeated aloud.

"He was my husband, you know," Aunt Abbie said. Jennifer wasn't sure if that was meant to be an answer, or not. She could well imagine that being Aunt Abbie's husband would be enough to make one angry. She could almost feel sorry for poor Wilfred.

"I think I'll go to my room," Jennifer said, completely disheartened. She was feeling the effects of her sleepless night. Her limbs felt leaden, and she knew that before she attempted to find her way again through the woods, she would have to rest.

"You missed breakfast, you know," Aunt Abbie called after her.

Jennifer continued on her way without answering. She made her way back to the front of the house. It was more than infuriating, it was maddening. Her senses were literally reeling from all that had happened. She was scratched and bruised from that headlong rush through the dense woods. And although she had found some little bit of food, it had hardly been enough. She still knew nothing about her car or its location, or for that matter, her location. She was tired and she was hungry. She was also angry, and more than a little frightened. She might have died in the woods, just as she might have died in the tower above the house.

Finding her way back here was little comfort. She could die in the house yet, the way things were going. Judging from what she had seen of the occupants of Kelsey House, no one would much care; if they even noticed, which was not likely. People who could make a meal of empty serving dishes, or watch as she fell and broke her neck, could just as easily carry on conversations with her empty chair while her starved corpse lay rotting in her bed.

CHAPTER TEN

It was evening when she awoke. The light that managed to find its way through the window of her room was all but gone. Jennifer's first realization was that she had slept through most of the day, after collapsing in exhaustion across her bed. She had not, she realized to her disgust, even taken the necessary time to pull back the spread, with the result that the front of her gray suit was now dismally black from the dirt that still clung to the spread.

"It can't matter much," she said unhappily, looking down at the suit. It was already so crumpled and torn that it would never again be restored to good looks.

After a moment's consideration, she decided she did not feel much better as a result of the extended nap. Her head was splitting and her hunger had developed into gnawing pains that began at her stomach and spread through her entire body. Even sitting up in the bed as she did now was an effort that sorely taxed her vanishing strength.

She looked again at the darkened window. Her spirits sank still lower as she realized she had slept the day away. The daylight was gone and she had intended to do something about her car. Now she would have to spend another night in this crazy house. And by morning, unless she found something to eat, her strength would be even further diminished. It seemed unlikely to her that she could even manage the walk back to her car, assuming she could find the way.

The door opened suddenly without advance warning. Jennifer turned her head in that direction, intending to snap at the intruder. To her delight, though, it was the young girl who had been beside her in the dining room, the one who had taken no part in the farce of eating. Slight as their bond was, Jennifer looked upon this child as the one genuinely friendly person in the place, and she was truly glad to see her now.

"I came to see if you were feeling better," the girl said, smiling brightly. There was something hauntingly sweet about the expression.

"I'm glad you did," Jennifer said, and meant it "Please do come in. I—I've forgotten your name."

"I'm Marcella."

"And I'm Jennifer. Would you like to sit down. The bed is the best I can offer; here, let me turn the spread back."

Marcella seated herself dutifully on a corner of the bed. "You don't mind my coming for a visit?" she asked.

"Mind? Heavens, you don't know what a relief it is to find someone sane in this house."

"I'm supposed to be with the others, but Aunt Christine said I could miss the rites for the evening."

"Oh, yes, the rites." Jennifer walked to the window and looked down upon the front lawn. There they were, the whole lot of them, doing their queer little dance again. It looked, she thought, not unlike a children's game; handholding and twirling about. Or a square dance, perhaps. But the impression was that it was more than just a game, or even a dance. There was some deeper significance to it she felt certain; religious symbolism, perhaps.

"What does it mean?" she asked, genuinely curious. If only she could begin to understand these people, the mysteries here might start clearing themselves up. Everything was so totally incomprehensible to her. She might as well be in a foreign country, she no more understood anyone here than if they were speaking a foreign tongue.

"Mean?" Marcella sounded puzzled by the question. "Why, it's the rites. The moon rites." She said it in such a tone of voice as to imply that that explained everything; probably, Jennifer thought, it does to her.

"Are you a relative too?" Jennifer asked, turning away from the window, back to her company. Curious though they might be, the rites could not help her get away from here. But Marcella might. She sensed a friendliness in the young girl's manner, and certainly Marcella did not behave like the others. Perhaps here, after all, was the ally she so badly needed.

It seemed almost impossible to believe that this sweet young thing was related to the other members of the household; but, she reminded herself unhappily, she was related to them herself. That was certainly a depressing fact.

"A relative of yours? Only a cousin, I think," Marcella said.

Jennifer sighed and said, "It's so difficult for me to get all these relatives straight in my mind, after so many years of thinking I hadn't any."

"Have you seen your mother?" Marcella asked when Jennifer paused.

Jennifer was startled; it was certainly a strange thing to ask. But the explanation was probably simple enough. As odd as the others in the household were, they had apparently neglected to explain her recent loss to this child. It was thoughtless of them, but not surprising.

"My mother is gone," she said quietly. She thought that the most tactful way of putting it.

Marcella however seemed to experience some difficulty in digesting that information, and Jennifer feared perhaps she had been too tactful. She was on the verge of rephrasing her explanation, but Marcella went off on another tack instead, to her surprise.

"Were you happy with her?" she asked.

Jennifer, who had been standing, seated herself on the opposite corner of the bed and thought about that question. It was one she had never actually considered before, not openly and fully. Had she been happy with her mother?

"To tell the truth," she said finally, "I don't think I know."

"You don't know?"

"Well, it's a little difficult for me to explain. She was a very strong woman, and a dominating one. I'm afraid I never really lived much of my own life, I just sort of shared hers, if that makes any sense. If I were happy or unhappy, I was merely sharing her emotions. She wanted me with her always. Everything I did was with, or for her. Sometimes I thought even my thoughts were hers."

Jennifer felt a little pang of guilt, discussing her mother this way, and with a girl she scarcely knew. And yet at the same time she experienced a sense of relief in doing so. She had never really had anyone to talk to before, never any opportunity to voice these thoughts that had so often crossed her mind, only to be pushed aside as disloyal and unfair.

She smiled wanly. "It isn't very easy to explain, I'm afraid. Even to myself," she said.

"Are you happier now?" Marcella asked.

Jennifer shook her head. "Since she died, you mean?" Marcella nodded. "I don't know that either," Jennifer said. "To tell you the truth, I don't guess I feel very much different. As I said, I never had a life, you see, and I don't suppose at this late stage of the game that I'll ever get around to having one. I could, I guess, but—oh, I don't know. I just don't really suppose she would want me to, somehow."

She reflected upon her statement for a moment. "There," she said, "that's what I mean. Gone or not, she hasn't stopped dominating me. Her life is gone, but she's still living mine for me. And to tell the truth, these last few days, I've wished she were here with me, to tell me what to do."

"But she is," Marcella said simply.

"Is what?"

"She is here."

Jennifer frowned. She was thinking of the empty chair at the dining room table, saved for her mother. Perhaps this cult the family belonged to touched upon the subject of death. She tried to think of a tactful way to reply to Marcella's comment.

"Yes, it's true, in a sense," she said, "that we're never parted from our loved ones. But only in a sense. And it isn't quite the same, don't you agree."

"How did she die?" Marcella asked, ignoring the question. "I mean, was it sudden, or did she...?"

"Did she know?" Jennifer finished the question that Marcella hesitated on; she was glad to see that the child did accept the idea of her mother being dead. "Yes, she knew for quite a while that it was coming, which is always a little more unpleasant. I've always thought I would rather go suddenly, not knowing."

"Still, knowing in advance gives you time to arrange everything."

"I suppose that's true. Anyway, we don't as a rule get to pick how we die."

Marcella leaned back, her hands behind her for support, and stared dreamily up at the ceiling with its paper flowers. "I was always frightened of drowning. I remember thinking how horrible it must be, with the water and the darkness and being so alone. But it wasn't that way at all."

"What wasn't what way?" Jennifer asked. She had been growing uneasy as the conversation progressed. It was a morbid subject in the first place, and although Marcella might well be the most sane person in the household, she still did make some peculiar remarks.

"It wasn't that way when I drowned," Marcella said matter-of-factly. "It wasn't horrible at all. It was like sleeping and dreaming. Someone, I think it was Mr. Hawthorne who said, 'We sometimes congratulate ourselves at the moment of waking from a troubled dream; it may be so the moment after death.' I felt like that. I heard music, strange music, unlike anything I had ever heard. And there were such lovely colors; not patterns or designs of any sort, just colors. And then the bad dream was over."

"You just fell into a lake and drowned, I suppose," Jennifer said a bit cuttingly. It didn't matter much if she offended Marcella on this subject. These were not very pleasant illusions for such a young girl to be having, and perhaps after all it would be as well to see them nipped in the bud, before she really did become as crazy as the rest of the family.

"I didn't fall into a lake. It was the stream, the one that runs through the woods. And as a matter of fact I didn't fall, my mother...."

"Marcella," Jennifer said sharply, interrupting the girl. She did not at all like the way this conversation was going, and she did not want to hear what role, in

Marcella's fantasy, her mother played in this drowning. "I...never mind all that. I need your help. Will you help me?"

"Oh, I should love to," Marcella cried, looking delighted at the prospect "What shall I help you to do; is it a secret?"

"Indeed it is a secret," Jennifer said, reminded to drop her voice to a whisper. "I want to leave Kelsey."

Marcella's jaw dropped, and her look of delight vanished at once. "But that isn't possible," she said, shaking her head solemnly.

"But it is," Jennifer cried, seizing the girl by her shoulders. "It must be."

"No one ever leaves," Marcella said. "But you'll grow to love it here. Everyone does."

Jennifer released her hold on Marcella's shoulders. She felt like crying in the face of this new opposition. "How can I love it here?" she said. "You've seen what's going on. You've no idea how terrible I feel, or how frightened I've been. I can't sleep. There's no food, and no water even to bathe."

"But there is water," Marcella said, seizing upon that mention. "There's a bathroom right through that door."

"Without water," Jennifer snapped. Didn't the child see the predicament she was in, without having to argue every detail with her. "I can't even wash my hands."

Marcella looked at her a bit doubtfully. "Aunt Christine says you just don't see things that are there," she said. "She says you'll get over that after a while, and then you'll be all right."

"But there isn't any water there," Jennifer cried aloud. "Come here, I'll show you."

Dutifully Marcella got up from the bed and went to the little bathroom with Jennifer. Jennifer twisted the taps violently. Nothing came from the faucets. She turned triumphant eyes on Marcella.

"There, you see," Marcella said. "There's plenty of water, just as I told you."

She was speaking exactly as if Jennifer were a child. She went to the sink, and began an elaborate panto-mime of washing her hands in the nonexistent stream of water.

"You see, we can wash our hands," she said in a sing song voice. "Let's wash our hands together, Cousin Jennifer, come on."

Jennifer began to cry. She couldn't help it, the tears came to her eyes and a great sob welled up in her throat. She turned and ran back to the bedroom, throwing herself across the bed, and cried brokenheartedly. What was she going to do? No one would help her, no one. And she was so tired and hungry.

After a time Marcella came and sat on the edge of the bed, and patted her shoulder. "There, there," she crooned in a low, musical voice. "It will be all right. You'll learn to love Kelsey."

"You don't understand," Jennifer sobbed. The sound of a sympathetic voice only made the tears come more abundantly. "I'm so hungry. I haven't had any food since I came."

"Well, that's certainly the truth," Marcella said.

Jennifer stopped sobbing and looked up into Marcella's concerned face. "It is?" she said. "I mean, you know that?"

"Why of course. I notice things. And I've been worried. I couldn't help thinking, she can't go very long without eating and not get sick."

Jennifer seized the girl's hands tightly. "Oh, Marcella, can you help me with that, at least? Can you get me some food? Please, I beg you, real food?"

"Why of course I can," Marcella said in a matter-of-fact tone. She pulled her hands gently free. "You just sit here and rest, and I'll see to it at once."

"You won't—won't forget?" Jennifer asked breathlessly. She could hardly believe, after all she had been through, that help was so readily available as this.

"No, I won't forget, not a second time."

"A second time?"

"I meant to bring some food with me when I came up, but I forgot. Aunt Christine tells me I'm the most thoughtless person she's ever encountered."

She got up and started from the room. At the door, she paused to say, "I was only fifteen at the time."

Jennifer, brushing the tears from her eyes, asked, "At what time?"

"When I drowned," Marcella said. She went out, closing the door softly.

That girl has been with these lunatics too long, Jennifer told herself; that's for sure. Perhaps, she added, it would be wise to take Marcella with her when she left Kelsey. Of course, before she made any plans of that sort, she would have to determine just how she was going to get away from the place. She didn't seem to be getting any closer to a solution.

Or was she? Marcella was willing to help. If she could convince the child of the danger she was in...and if she suggested that Marcella come with her. Was that kidnapping? Well, it could hardly matter. Hadn't she been virtually kidnapped herself, kept a prisoner here? No, the family surely would not want to make a police matter of all this. And it would be best for Marcella.

She lifted her eyes and caught sight of herself in the dusty mirror over the dresser.

"I am a sight," she said. The scratches from her morning in the woods had turned livid, and there were smears of dried blood on her face and arms. Her suit was almost literally a shambles, and she was covered with filth. She looked like a wild woman; she scarcely recognized herself in that savage reflection.

The minutes seemed to drag by. She had nearly decided that Marcella had lied to her, when a soft knock came at the door. She rushed to it, flinging it open. "Oh, Marcella," she exclaimed, and then caught herself.

It was not Marcella, but Aunt Abbie who stood outside, holding the familiar silver tray before her. She smiled disarmingly. "Marcella said you wanted something to eat," she said. "So I've brought you a tray up. I'm glad to know you're feeling hungry at last."

Jennifer watched mutely as Aunt Abbie brought the tray into the room and set it atop the dresser.

"Now you enjoy your meal," Aunt Abbie said, starting from the room again. "And then you'll feel better. It isn't good to skip meals."

Jennifer stood motionless for several moments after she had gone. Then, although she felt sure of what she would find, she crossed slowly to the dresser and lifted the lid from the silver tray.

It was empty, of course. She nearly screamed aloud, or threw the tray at the wall. They were trying to starve her, it was obvious; or drive her mad; or both.

But why? How much money had her mother left her, a few thousand? Certainly it was not a fortune.

But of course her relatives would have no idea how much it amounted to. Was it possible that they somehow had a mistaken idea that it was more? Perhaps they thought she was rich, and that she stood between them and a fortune. Was it conceivable that they were doing these things to her for the sake of gaining an inheritance?

Anything was conceivable. She might not have thought that a short time before, but she had learned that lesson at least in her stay so far at Kelsey House. Much of her thinking had had to be changed.

She looked about the room, at the furnishings, ugly and dismal, at the horrid wallpaper, at the dirt everywhere. Impulsively she tore the slip from one of the bedpillows and began to dust frantically, running the cloth with ferocious movements over the dresser, the stool, even the floor. She worked as if possessed by demons, and the dust rose in the air like a fog, filling her nostrils, wrapping itself about her in little wisps, only to settle again as thickly as before. Tears streaming down her face left little white trails through the black that smeared her cheeks.

At last with a small sob she threw herself across the bed again, clenching the now black cloth tightly in one hand.

* * * * * * *

Lydia. Aunt Lydia. In her sleep, the name reverberated through her mind.

"We had hoped Lydia would be with us.... She'll join us soon...."

That was what Aunt Christine had said. A simple enough remark to make. Why should it haunt her so, as it did? Why did that name linger in her mind? There was something her mother had said at some time about Aunt Lydia. That, and the image of a letter. The memory teetered on the brink of her consciousness, and then was gone.

"Jennifer."

Her name again. But it was not here, at Kelsey. She was at home, in her bed, the bed that had been moved into her mother's sickroom. She was living again the long weeks before her mother's death. Agonizing, sleepless nights, a constant vigil at her mother's side, long days of exhaustion; and medicines to prolong both of their labors.

"Jennifer."

It was that night again, the night of her mother's

death, and she was so weary, so very tired. She was asleep, deeply, heavily asleep, and the name had invaded her sleep. It came, the calling, and grew more plaintive and more distant, weaker and still weaker. She had awakened, or half awakened, but her sleep had been too deep. She had drifted off again, not to awaken again until morning, to find....

"No, I didn't hear my name," she argued, burying her face in her pillow. "I dreamed it. You didn't call."

Her voice became a whimper. The dream faded and passed away.

CHAPTER ELEVEN

Morning. Another morning at Kelsey House. How many had there been so far? The days had run together in a bewildering stream, so that she no longer knew how long she had been here. A week? Surely not that long, but she could not say for certain.

She rose, peering out on the lawn, and there was Mr. Kelsey, Aunt Christine's husband, standing by himself below her window. Mr. Kelsey who had not yet spoken a word to her. Was he as mad as the rest, or was he, in some way, a prisoner like herself? She had observed that he felt no affection toward the women of the household, and Aunt Christine had suggested as much. Perhaps he too wanted to leave. If only he would help her find her car, she would be more than happy to take him along with her when she left. She would take any of them along, any and all, if they would only allow her to go.

She must try to enlist Mr. Kelsey's help. Surely someone among all the people in this house must regret what was being done to her. They couldn't all be monsters who could enjoy watching her starve to death, or go mad, without lifting a hand to help her.

She left her room and made her way quickly down the stairs to the main hall, and the entrance. The sun was warm and soothing when she came out, the air mellow. It was a lovely autumn day. It was certainly not the sort of day that one ought to be trapped in a house that defied comprehension, desperately alone.

He was still there on the lawn, exactly where she had seen him from her window. He stood motionless and stared across the lawn in the direction of the woods beyond. She thought he looked at them with longing, and the possibility that he too might want to leave seemed even stronger. He gave no indication that he heard her approach until she stood almost beside him.

"Good morning," she greeted him, sounding as cheerful as she could manage. She did not want to offend him or turn him away from her. But she could not quite keep the note of desperation from creeping into her voice.

He turned, his eyes meeting hers, and for an instant all hope died in her breast. She had an urge to run, to leave him at once. What was it, that look that he gave her? Hatred? Violence, surely—no, nothing as active as that. A coldness, a terrible, lifeless emptiness that sent an involuntary shudder through her.

He turned away from her again almost at once, looking back toward the woods. It was as though he had dismissed her.

She would not be put off so easily, however. She summoned her courage again and said, "It certainly is a beautiful day, isn't it?"

He made no answer, nor did he even acknowledge her comment but only continued to stare into the distance. Courtesy, Jennifer thought was not encouraged here at Kelsey.

"I'm afraid I haven't been able to find my car," she continued, determined to make the effort to enlist his aid. "I wonder if you could tell me how to find that road again, the road that the stream crosses."

Still he ignored her.

"I do think you could at least answer me," she snapped angrily.

Still he did not reply. Without even looking again in her direction, he turned and started back toward the front porch of the house. She watched as he climbed the steps and passed through the door.

"Well, that beats everything," she declared aloud, staring after him.

"He can't talk, you know."

The voice came from behind her. Jennifer whirled about, startled. It was disconcerting, to say the least, the way these people crept up on you without any warning.

"He can't talk," Marcella repeated, smiling at her.

"That's no excuse," Jennifer said, too angry and frustrated to feel sympathetic or charitable. "He could have at least made some sign to me that he heard me. Or can't he hear either?"

"Oh, his hearing is fine. But he's never forgiven Aunt Christine for what she did, and it's made him rather distant, I think."

Yes, Aunt Christine had said something similar herself—"Wilfred has never forgiven me...."

"What did Aunt Christine do?" she asked.

"She had his tongue pulled out," Marcella informed her cheerfully. "That's why he can't talk. I'm afraid it was too much for his heart. He...."

"Marcellal!" Jennifer stared at her in horror. Was this only another example of the girl's vivid imagination, or was she telling the truth? Surely Aunt Christine could not really have done such a thing. "You can't mean what you're saying."

"Oh yes," Marcella said, looking taken aback that her statement had been questioned. "I watched."

"But that...that's terrible."

"Yes, it was. Quite terrible."

Jennifer stared open-mouthed. Her mind was reeling from the shock of what she had just been told. What kind of monsters were these people, these relatives she had once been so eager to meet? What form of madness could devise so dreadful a deed?

But it went beyond that. Until now, she had clung to the hope, however faint, that there was some awful mistake going on. She had not fully believed that these people could truly mean to let her starve; she had been sure within herself that no one could be that cruel. Now she saw that it was madness to cling to that hope. If Aunt Christine could have her own husband's tongue taken out she would certainly not hesitate to let a niece die of starvation.

"Marcella," she said, her voice hoarse and strained,

"Marcella we must leave here. You must go with me, and help me find my car, and we will go away from this terrible place, just the two of us."

"Oh, I can't leave here," Marcella replied. "It isn't allowed."

"But you can, and you must," Jennifer insisted. "It's not safe here, can't you understand that. All we have to do is find my car. You must know your way through the woods. I'll go up now and get my purse, the car keys are in it, and we can leave at once."

"Aunt Christine would never allow me to leave," Marcella said, seeming quite unalarmed at the prospect of danger.

"But we won't tell her," Jennifer said. "It will be our secret, and by the time they discover that we've gone, we can be miles from here. All we need to do is find my car, and it will be all right."

"But it is all right," Marcella said. "There's no need for us to leave."

"But...."

"Good morning."

Jennifer turned to find Aunt Christine standing nearby, only a few feet away. How long, she wondered fearfully, had the woman been standing there? How much of the conversation had she heard?

CHAPTER TWELVE

It did not seem as if Aunt Christine had overheard Jennifer's grim conversation with Marcella. The older woman's smile was as cheerful and whimsical as ever. Jennifer met her eyes, and found herself trying to envision that horrible scene that Marcella had mentioned. Could this smiling old woman who looked so frail and harmless actually have had her husband's tongue pulled out? No, it seemed impossible that Aunt Christine could do anything so terrible, mad though she might be.

And yet, Jennifer reminded herself, here I am, starving to death; and for all I know, my tongue may be next to go. She can't like some of the things I've been saying.

Aloud, she said, "Excuse me."

Aunt Christine made no attempt to stop or delay her, and when she had started toward the house, she heard her Aunt and Marcella begin to talk in voices too low for her to hear what was being said.

She supposed Aunt Christine must have heard some of their conversation, and was now badgering the child for more details. Jennifer half expected to be attacked before she reached the house. But nothing happened. She reached the safety of the porch, and entered the house, walking without pause up the wide stairway. Not until she had reached the relative safety of her own room with the door locked after her did she stop.

She sank wearily down upon the bed. "I must remain calm," she told herself, but in truth she felt anything but calm. She knew she must try again to leave Kelsey House.

"But to begin with, I must find some food," she said. It would be impossible for her to do much of anything unless she found some food, and found it soon. And even if she did not leave, she might need some strength. She might have to defend herself.

There had to be a logical way of looking at all that had happened. "Everything," her mother had been fond of saying, "makes sense, in its own way. Sometimes you have to discover what sort of sense it makes." So far, things at Kelsey did not seem to make sense. But that was because she had not yet discovered what sort of sense they did make.

To begin with, they had to eat and keep themselves alive. They all looked healthy enough, that was for sure. So, that meant they must be eating when she was not with them. They had plenty of opportunities. Perhaps she could catch them at it.

That idea, though, seemed less appealing the more she thought of it. There were too many of them, and she had no reason to suppose they ate together. She could not follow them all around all day long.

Perhaps she could pick a likely spot and just wait until she found someone there eating. If she hid herself in the dining room, for instance....

Upon reflection, the dining room seemed unlikely. There had been no evidence, on her trips there, to suggest that anyone had eaten anything there in years—no spilled crumbs, no food stains.

She went back to the idea of following people—of following one person. Perhaps if she followed Aunt Christine, for instance.

She gave her head a shake. No, she couldn't follow her everywhere. Suppose Aunt Christine ate in the privacy of her room. Suppose the food arrived some secret way, by dumbwaiter or through another corridor. This house might well have that sort of convenience.

She abandoned the idea of finding them eating. She would have to work on finding food. There certainly was an indisputable fact; they had to have food. There had to be food in the house somewhere.

The answer came to her in a flash. The kitchen, of course. There would certainly be food in the kitchen. More than likely, this was where they ate too. Old houses like this often had huge kitchens, with tables set up there. She could almost envision the kitchen, warm and cheery, filled with the smells of bread baking and something spicy simmering atop the stove. There would be a big old table, round, and made of oak, or perhaps maple. From time to time during the day, perhaps even now, at this moment, various members of the family gathered over coffee and hot plates of steaming food.

While they ate they talked, perhaps they laughed at the plight of their house guest, and planned how they would behave toward her at evening, when they pantomimed dinner in the dining room.

Her vision was so real that she nearly smelled the food and heard their voices. Her mouth actually began to water.

"I must find the kitchen," she told herself. There was the obvious solution.

But at once her spirits sank again. How was she to find it? At the very least, that meant another trip through the house, and probably getting lost again. How on earth did people find their ways about in unfamiliar places? Men had explored the globe—the continents, and the ocean floors, even the jungles. They had gone through space and back. And she couldn't find her way through a crumbling old house. Surely if she thought calmly and clearly, some means would occur to her. Not a map, no. Nor a compass.

"A string," she said aloud, her face brightening. Yes, that was it of course, they carried a string with them and left a trail for themselves to follow. She remembered a story in which children had left a trail of breadcrumbs. In that, though, the crumbs had been eaten by birds, so that their trail had vanished. Well, she was not going to leave crumbs, and anyway, there were no birds inside the house, not of the feathered variety anyway.

She frowned again. Where was she to find a string long enough to leave a trail for herself to follow? Without much hope of finding anything, she opened a drawer of the dresser. It was empty, as was the second one that she opened. But she did find something in the third—not a string, but a spool of white thread. A spool of thread would do as well, perhaps even better.

She went out into the hall, taking the thread with her. There was no one in sight, not in the upstairs hall, nor in the downstairs hall. She thought as she descended the stairs that she should have looked from her window to see if there was anyone on the lawn. Aunt Christine had been there a short time before, and Marcella. But she saw no one in the house. In fact, now that she thought of it, it was difficult to imagine where all of these people spent their time; she so seldom saw any of them. Surely they did not just spend their entire days in their rooms.

Kelsey was a large house, however, and it was obvious that the part of it she saw was not where the family spent their time. There must be another section of the house in which they lived; rooms, perhaps, in which they played bridge or cribbage, or read.

In her mind, she saw rooms with open fireplaces and walls of books, and on a tray would be a decanter of sherry and several dainty little glasses. There would be a rustling as the pages were turned in books, and perhaps the clink of glasses, and a crackling from the fire, and from time to time the clicking of knitting needles. Oh, if only they would invite her in there. How happy she would be with such a simple homely scene.

She came to the downstairs hall and walked instinctively to the front. There she paused outside the first door. This was the room in which she had waited for Aunt Christine, and from which she had started before. She had found nothing that way, not even evidence that anyone else used that part of the house. Perhaps it would be better if she started on the other side of the hall. After all, somewhere in this monstrous house there had to be those rooms they used for their living quarters. If they were not on one side of the hall, then they must be on the other.

She opened the door directly across the hall and peered in, half expecting to see the whole family sitting there, the pack of them, waiting for her to find them, waiting to laugh.

The room was another sitting room, similar to several she had seen already, and it was empty, so far as people went. There was plenty of furniture, and it wore the same coating of filth she had seen elsewhere.

She stepped inside, allowing the door to swing shut behind her. Then, very carefully, she tied one end of her white thread to the knob, tying several knots so that it could not accidentally come loose. This time she would take no chances.

Satisfied that her thread was secure, she started out from the room she was in, holding the spool in her hand and trailing the string behind her.

The rooms she saw were not much different from the ones she had seen the time before. When had that been? A day ago? A week ago? She really had no idea; time did not seem to flow in its natural course here.

Nothing here seemed to flow in its natural course.

And all these rooms, so much alike, serving no particular purpose. Whoever had designed the house originally (Aunt Christine had told her: Robert Kelsey, wasn't it) had been interested first and foremost in size, judging from all appearances. A lot of rooms had been the first requirement and no one seemed to have cared whether the rooms were of any use.

She passed through room after room, always choosing, if there were a choice, the exit that seemed to offer the straightest path.

"This time," she told herself firmly, "I am not going to travel in a circle." She was sure of this, and it followed that even if she found nothing, she was certain to reach the end of the house eventually, even if it took her all day.

And that, she realized, was another oddity. In the other part of the house, the part she had explored previously, she had apparently followed the outside walls of the house; most of the rooms had had windows, so far as she remembered. The rooms she was in now were, without exception, windowless. Either her trail was taking her directly through the house without approaching the extremities, which was entirely possible, or one side of the house had been built without windows; quite possible in this strange house.

The result of this oddity was that despite the bright sunlight outside, the rooms were dark as night. Without thinking she had taken to turning on the lights as she entered each room, leaving them on behind her. It was, she thought, like traveling through a nether world of night and darkness; indeed, the very shadows around her seemed alive, hovering about her, watching and listening. She shivered at the thought and tried to laugh at herself, but the laugh was unconvincing.

"You're really going crazy," she said, speaking instinctively in a whisper.

It was difficult to keep track of time here, and so she did not know just how long she had been walking. Nor did she know when or how the thread had broken. No doubt she had caught it carelessly on one of the doors as she passed through. But broken it was, the end of it trailing behind her. For a moment panic nearly overcame her again.

"Now wait," she cautioned herself, fighting down the sense of helplessness that threatened to engulf her. "I have been unwinding this the whole time. If that's all the tail there is hanging from the spool, it must have just broken. If it had broken very far back, I would be dragging yards and yards of it after me, instead of just a few inches here."

She remained outwardly calm. She backtracked, reentering the room she had just left, watching the floor for the telltale thread. But there was no thread here. Across the room were two doors, almost side by side. Try though she might, she could not remember which one she had come through.

Heart in throat, she approached them and opened the first one, peering beyond. There was no thread there either. Closing that one, she opened the other. Still no thread. She closed that door also, before she thought of the lights.

She had turned on the lights on her way through the house, and that should have left another trail for her to follow; but both of the rooms she had just looked into were lighted.

She thought of Hansel and Gretel, and their trail of crumbs that the birds had eaten. Well, certainly no bird had come along to eat her thread.

But it had certainly vanished.

"This is ridiculous," she said aloud, the sound of her own voice startling her. "There were no lights on when I came through. And anyway, I could not have come this far since the thread broke."

Unless, she thought, and this thought she did not voice aloud, unless someone had turned on the lights, had removed the thread, someone following her from room to room, watching her, as the shadows in the corner were watching her....

She shuddered violently. On an impulse she returned to the room where she had discovered that the thread was broken. There was only one other door in this room. Perhaps as before she would find that she had made her way back to the main hall.

The door was locked, however. It was the first one she had found that was locked, and that alone was enough to make her suspicious, but that was not all. At almost the same moment that she tried the knob, she heard a sound from the other side, a sound that might have been a smothered cough.

No, she amended her thoughts, this was not the first locked door she had found. There had been one that other morning she had gotten lost in the house, a door that had seemed to lock itself. And she had thought there was someone beyond that door too; she was convinced of it now.

The truth came to her suddenly. She had found what she had been seeking, the kitchen; that was why this room, of all the rooms in the house, was locked to her. She was at the kitchen door and someone was on the other side of this door, waiting for her to leave. Perhaps it was the person who did the cooking. Perhaps it was more than one person. She saw again the big oak table she had imagined earlier, saw the family sitting about it, food before them, their forks poised en route to their mouths. They sat with eyes turned in this direction, saying nothing, listening.

With stubborn courage she raised one fist and knocked loudly on the door. There was no response.

"Open this door," she demanded, desperation giving her unusual bravado. They were not going to fool her by merely pretending they were not there. She would get through this door if she had to break it down.

Whoever was beyond the door coughed again.

"What gall!" she thought. They were not even trying to keep their presence a secret now. More than likely they were all there, the whole family, beyond this door, and they were laughing at her, laughing at her desperate demands.

With rising anger and frustration she pounded again,

first with one fist and then with the other, and then with both of them as her emotions overcame her and she began to sob.

"Please, please, let me in," she cried, sinking to her knees before the oak door. She was so weak from hunger, and so miserable, even her reason seemed to be escaping her.

No, no it wasn't only the hunger, or the events that had taken place, or her unhappiness. She had grown cold, frightfully cold, and so weak that she could scarcely lift her hands to the door, let alone pound on its surface. And her mind was indeed slipping away from her, it seemed as if she could feel it go, moving out of her, into time and infinite space.

"This is insane," she told herself, shaking her head as if to clear the clouds from her consciousness. "I've never felt like this before."

In terror she tried to stand, or to scream, and she was suddenly aware that she was fainting, aware of the blackness rushing in upon her. Her last memory was of a sound, the sound of metal against metal. The sound of a key turning in a lock.

CHAPTER THIRTEEN

It was night and she was there again, the woman in the white robe, the woman with the long dark hair. She hovered over the bed, bending down to peer at closer range. Jennifer tried to be frightened. She knew she should be frightened, but she felt nothing. Her mind and her senses failed to function at her command. She remembered wondering idly if they were going to kill her in her bed. How easy that would be for them, much easier and faster than what they were doing. She could not stop them. She would not even try.

She felt the same awesome chill that she had felt when she fainted. Perhaps, she thought, I'm dead already. Perhaps I have been dead for a long time. How would she know?

There it was again, her name. She heard her name being called. The night of her mother's death came back to her then, fleetingly and grimly.

"Jennifer." The name, pleading and faint

"Aunt Lydia...." The voice was Aunt Christine's. No, not Aunt Christine's at all, but another voice, familiar. She tried to focus her attention on that voice. "Aunt Lydia...Aunt Lydia has...."

And then it was morning, and she was awake, and the nightmares had gone. She was in her bed, in her room with the faded wallpaper and the velvet drapes. For a moment she did not know how she had come to be here. Then her memory came back, in little patches, like clouds scudding before the wind. Her journey through the house, the broken thread, the door. And her fainting.

Someone had brought her here, had undressed her and put her to bed. But who? Certainly not any of the women, nor Mr. Kelsey, frail old thing that he was. But Mr. Kelsey was the only man in the house with the exception of Wilfred, the hired man.

No, not a hired man, she reminded herself, but Aunt Abbie's husband. For an instant she imagined his eyes, brutal and cold, staring into hers. She shuddered at the possibility that he might have put her to bed, and quickly forced the thought from her mind.

She turned her head, looking about the room. She was surprised to see Aunt Abbie there, at the dresser again, fumbling with the air about the empty flower vase. She looked up as if she knew Jennifer was now looking in her direction, and smiled brightly.

"Good morning," she said. She sounded quite cheerful; just as if, Jennifer thought, just as if it were really a good morning. As though nothing at all out of the ordinary were happening.

Or was it, she asked herself, out of the ordinary? Ordinary for whom?

I am losing my mind, she thought.

"Have you ever seen such beautiful colors in roses?" Aunt Abbie asked, seemingly unaware of the fact that Jennifer had failed to return her greeting. Or perhaps, Jennifer thought, she thought she had heard a greeting. She saw things that were not there; why not hear things that weren't ever said.

Jennifer stared in silence at the older woman. It was clear that Aunt Abbie thought there were roses in the vase, roses she had brought from her own garden. They were as plain to Aunt Abbie as the food that they served for their meals, the food that wasn't there.

But if that were the case, perhaps the food was not a joke, or a plot to starve her to death, or drive her crazy. Perhaps they really saw it. Perhaps it was really there.

In which case, they have driven me crazy, Jennifer thought It was a maddening circle that closed in upon her with each passing second.

"Breakfast will be ready in a few minutes," Aunt Abbie informed her. She smiled again and went out.

Jennifer raised one hand weakly to her forehead. Her face felt warm to the touch; she had a fever. It was no wonder, with all she had been through, and with the lack of food. How long had it been since she had eaten anything? She couldn't even remember. Even her memory seemed to be failing her. And it was entirely possible she had caught something, a cold, or even pneumonia. She was not a strong person. She had always been highly susceptible to things; her mother had told her that. Weak as she was, she would never survive getting sick now. Even a simple cold would probably be too much for her weakened condition.

But what could she do? Marcella had been her best hope, and she now believed that Marcella was as strange as the rest. Even granting that the child meant well by her, she was too frightened to help her escape. What else could she do? Who could she turn to for help?

There was still Wilfred, Aunt Abbie's husband. He was different from the others, in some way she could not yet understand. He was apart from them. He took no part in any of the activities about the house, at least so far as she could see. She had never seen him at any of those charade meals in the dining room. He had in fact rescued her twice, in a manner of speaking. Perhaps she should try to enlist his aid again.

But he was not really much of a possibility. From the way he looked at her, he would as soon see her dead.

"If I had food," she said again, "I might be able to escape." Even wandering through the woods for a time now seemed preferable to staying here. Sooner or later she must surely come to a road or another house, or some sign of life.

But without food she would not last out a night in her present condition. She should have left before, risked that escape without food, before she got so terribly weak. Now it seemed hopeless. What if she fainted, as she had done the night before?

That scene came back to her. The locked door, and the presence beyond it, waiting, listening. And later, in her room, the figure bending over her, the dark haired visitor who came to her room.

The memory sent a shiver through her. That at least she would find a means to stop. She might well be a prisoner here; indeed, at this juncture she could hardly consider herself anything else. But she would not have anyone in this house hovering over her while she slept.

She slept again after that. It was afternoon when she awoke once more, and her fever had grown worse. She was unquestionably sick and getting sicker.

"I am going to die in this house," she thought in numb horror. "I am going to die here, in this dirty bed, in this gruesome room and no one will ever know."

She remembered then that there was no one who should know anyway, no one even to be informed. She had no friends, no relatives, except for the people in this house with her, no one who would care one way or another.

She sat up in the bed, reaching toward the floor where she had left her purse at nights. Instead of the cool smoothness of the leather purse, her fingers touched the rough wood surface of the floor. She moved her hand about groping along the floor for the purse.

She stood up, looking about the room frantically. Her purse was gone.

That meant everything she had was gone too. Her keys to the car, her money. It wasn't her money, though, that they had wanted. She would happily have given that to them. There had not been much of it, and furthermore they could have just taken it from the purse, at any of several opportunities. The keys were more logical, the keys to her car. Perhaps they meant to steal the car and sell it somewhere.

No, not sell it. But it was a way of insuring that she remained here without any means of escape. There was always the possibility she might find her way back to the car; but without her keys, that would do her no good.

Still, they could have as easily just taken the keys from her purse. No, it was something more than the keys or the money.

She thought she understood after a moment. The purse had been the only thing she had with her. Aside from the filthy, torn suit she wore, it was her only link to the world of the past the life she had known before Kelsey House. It was, in a frightening sense, *her*. Her total identity. It was her memory, her past. Her life.

It was the final evidence of her separateness from them. And it was gone.

CHAPTER FOURTEEN

The discovery that her purse was missing made her angry again, and with anger came a renewing of her strength. She had had enough. She meant to confront her Aunt Christine and flatly demand that she be allowed to leave Kelsey House. She had been robbed and frightened and humiliated and starved, and no one, not even a madwoman, could expect her to remain.

At least she had her suit left. It was still there, in the armoire, where she usually hung it. At least whoever had put her to bed last night (and she did not want to think about that) had not thought to steal her clothing. Although there on the bed was that silly white robe they wanted her to wear. On that point she would be firm. If it meant sleeping in her suit, they would not get it away from her; and she would not, under any circumstances, wear that robe.

Not, she thought bitterly when she had donned it, that it could be called presentable. It was filthy and torn and horribly wrinkled. The very sight of it on herself filled her with disgust

She was, in fact, as filthy herself as the suit was. She had never thought before how essential cleanliness was to a sense of well-being, nor how demoralizing dirt could be.

She used a corner of the sheet to try to rub some of the dirt from her face; the result was a grotesque streaking of the dust that made her look as if she were made up for some tasteless masquerade. Her comb and makeup were in her purse, so that she could do nothing more than brush her hair back with her fingers. The efforts were rather pathetically wasted. When she was done she looked at her reflection in the mirror.

I look a fright, she thought with a grimace. It is difficult to be authoritative when you look like a street urchin. But there was nothing more she could do; she left her room.

Marcella was just coming up the stairs, bearing the familiar gleaming tray. "I was bringing your breakfast up to you," she greeted her, stopping in front of Jennifer. "You missed that and lunch too. I hope you're feeling better than you were."

Jennifer stared hard at the lid on the tray, fighting the temptation to lift it and look inside. Marcella looked so sweet and friendly; and Jennifer almost thought she could smell the aroma of warm food drifting to her nostrils. It smelled like bacon, crisp from the frying, and eggs.

She swallowed, and fought back the impulse. That was futile, she knew only too well. Her senses were playing tricks on her, with smells of bacon and eggs. Her own mind could no longer be trusted. The dishes would be as empty as they had been before, and she would only be that more demoralized for having believed once again.

Instead, she asked, "Where will I find Aunt Christine?"

"In her room," Marcella answered simply.

"Where on earth is her room?" Jennifer demanded, frightened even at the thought of another search through this house.

Marcella nodded her head toward the hall behind her. "It's the room next to yours."

"Thank you," Jennifer said, turning and starting back down the hall.

"Aren't you hungry?" Marcella called after her.

Jennifer came to a stop, clenching her hands into fists. I am going to take that tray, she thought savagely, and...she left the thought unfinished and took a deep breath. No temper. Remain calm. She mustn't lose her head again, she must remain calm and in full control of herself. And anyway, losing her temper and screaming at Marcella would tire her further, and that she especially could not afford. She must conserve her strength. Somehow she would escape, and she would need all of her strength. It was precious little as it was; she could not risk wasting any of it.

She went on her way, calmer again. She little cared whether Marcella followed her or not but she glanced back once to see that the girl had started back down the stairs with the tray.

"At least now they know I'm not going to go along with that nonsense anymore," she told herself. She passed by her own door and paused outside the one next to it. She raised her hand to knock, and hesitated.

There were voices inside the room. She couldn't tell through the heavy door what was being said, but there was more than one voice. Aunt Christine was not alone. There was someone with her, and they were talking; maybe even talking about her.

She leaned closer, finally pressing herself against the door, trying to hear. Two voices, that she was sure of, and both of them belonging to women.

"...her food," one of them said. The other said something in reply that included the word, "Jennifer."

They were talking about her, and about food! Jennifer pressed closer against the door, trying to hear, but the words remained muffled and indistinct.

She thought of the keyhole then, and quickly knelt. She put her eye to it but the scene she saw within was too limited—nothing more than a corner of a writing table, and a fragment of what looked like a chair.

Nor was she able to hear very much better through the keyhole. She caught her name again, and after a bit a reference to Marcella.

She stiffened, sure that they were discussing her conversation on the lawn with Marcella. They did know, then, that she was trying to escape, and had begged Marcella for aid; had suggested, in fact, that Marcella come with her.

If only they would raise their voices.

Uncomfortable in her kneeling position, she put her hand out to brace herself. It brushed the doorknob, which rattled. At once the voices within grew silent

Jennifer jumped quickly to her feet watching the door and expecting it to open. But there was only silence that went on until she grew uneasy.

At last unable to remain inactive, she knocked at the door. At once Aunt Christine's voice called out: "Who is it?"

"It's Jennifer," she called back, a little louder than should have been necessary. "I want to come in."

"Why, by all means. The door is unlocked."

The door was indeed unlocked. Jennifer came in, to find Aunt Christine seated on a small rocker before a tea table. On the table a silver tea service glittered brightly. Across the table from Aunt Christine was a small divan, but it was empty. Aunt Christine was alone in the room.

Jennifer looked slowly about the room, confirming the fact. There was only the one door, the one through which she had come, and there was no one else present in this room.

She walked slowly to the tea table, looking down at the service. Yes, there were two cups of tea poured. There was one directly in front of Aunt Christine, and across the table from her, in front of the divan, was another cup, half-empty. As she seated herself at the divan, Jennifer let her hand brush the cup ever so slightly. The cup was still warm. Someone had been here, had finished half a cup of tea, had been talking with Aunt Christine not more than a minute before; and was not here now.

Or was hiding she added. She glanced about again. The room did not afford too many places to conceal oneself; under the bed perhaps, or in the armoire.

Or perhaps Aunt Christine customarily drank two cups of tea at a time and talked to herself while she did so. It was peculiar, but not really any more peculiar than a great many other things about the place.

"I hope you're feeling better," Aunt Christine was saying. "You gave us a fright, you know, fainting the way you did."

"I haven't been sleeping well," Jennifer answered. Now, she was thinking, now is the time to have it out with her. Instead, she said, "Aunt Abbie has been in my room, you know."

"Yes, she asked if she might bring you some roses in the mornings. She's so proud of her flowers. I told her it would be all right."

"Roses? Oh yes, the roses." Jennifer passed a hand over her eyes. It seemed that there should be something more than this to discuss, but her thoughts were so scattered by this time.

I must get out of here, she told herself. I must do something. I must tell her I want to leave this house immediately or I will...I will what?

"Will you please ask Aunt Abbie not to come into my room in the future? In fact, would you please ask everyone to stay out of my room altogether?"

Aunt Christine seemed appropriately shocked by this request, but she said hastily, "Why of course dear, if that's what you want. It is your room."

She recovered quickly, and said, "Won't you have some tea?"

"No, no thank you," Jennifer murmured. She knew that if she was ever to take a stand, it must be now, this very minute. She must make her position perfectly clear. Aunt Christine should know that she was not a fool, that she had not been taken in by any of what had happened.

But it was just as before; the words would not come. There was the same awful sensation of being not in control, not even of her own faculties. She felt as if her mind were not her own. And she had grown cold again; not just suddenly, either. It had come upon her since she had entered the room, that terrible coldness that she had experienced before. Starting slowly, then increasing until she felt made of ice. It was like death, so absolute, so total.

"I'm hungry," she said plaintively. "So very hungry."

Somehow she had gotten to her feet. Her ears were roaring loudly. Something is wrong, she thought. I must get out of this room at once.

"I can't be surprised," Aunt Christine was saying, as if from afar off. "Why, you've not touched a bite of food since you came. It's no wonder you feel poorly."

Jennifer scarcely heard the words. She was not even in Kelsey House. She was a child again, and she was at home. Her mother was scolding her for gobbling her food down.

"The way you eat, Jennifer, you would think missing one meal would kill you for sure. And your manners are dreadful. I shall punish you in the future by making you go without supper."

And she had done just that, whenever Jennifer was bad; which meant whenever Jennifer had expressed an idea of her own, or had taken any pleasure of her own in anything, or kept anything to herself.

"Please," she said aloud, stumbling toward the door. "Tell Aunt Abbie to stay out of my room."

She stumbled into the hall, hardly able to walk or stand. She did not know what had come over her, but she had to flee that room, had to flee Aunt Christine's presence. Her own room suddenly seemed a welcome haven.

She went to it, locking the door, and fell weakly across her bed. Not until then did she think of the cup of tea her Aunt had offered her.

It had been tea. There had been tea, warm tea, in the cup on the table! It had not been empty, nor a pretense, but real tea!

She began to laugh then, a horrid, desperate sound that became sobs. She was losing her mind; perhaps she had already lost it. They were winning, and she was helpless to fight them.

The sobs continued as she fell asleep, and even in her sleep she continued to cry softly, until she felt comforting arms about her shoulders, soft hands stroking her brow, soothing her. Slowly, ever so slowly, the sobs subsided, and she was calm again for a time, allowing herself to be comforted.

She was not asleep! The realization swept over her.

She was awake, and it was night and she was in someone's arms. With a shriek she leaped up from the bed.
She stumbled over the stool, falling face down on the
floor. She screamed, again and again, and no one came;
nothing happened.

Finally, her throat raw from screaming, she sat up,
still trembling. The bed was empty. She stood, stumbling to the switch by the door, and bathed the room in
light. There was no one in the room. She tried the door
and found it locked, just as she had left it.

"Oh, my God," she said aloud. In her terror she could
still feel the arms about her shoulders, the hands at her
face. "Oh my God."

CHAPTER FIFTEEN

It was another full day before Jennifer was well enough to leave her room again. She slept in fitful snatches fully clothed in her shabby gray suit. The light, harsh and glaring, burned constantly overhead. The door remained locked, and she had even managed the strength necessary to push the dresser across the room. It now stood in front of the door, blockading the room.

At least a dozen times Aunt Christine had knocked at the door and called to her from the hall, but she had stubbornly refused to answer.

Let them worry, let them think what they like, she told herself.

Twice someone else knocked without identifying who it was.

Her sleep was crowded with dreams, some of them terrifying, all of them strange; brief scenes that flashed through her mind without order or pattern. Her mother; Aunt Lydia's name; things that had happened at Kelsey; locked doors and faceless women; and something about a letter.

Where had the letter come from, and what did it

mean?

She saw it clearly in her dreams, a neat little note-paper that floated just beyond her reach. She felt, in her sleep, that if she could only reach out, grasp it and read the words scrawled upon it, that everything, all of the queer events that had brought her to this state, would suddenly be clear. But the letter eluded her, floating just out of her reach.

In her dream she raced up and down stairways, climbing into the turret, with its broken walkway. She came in and out of locked rooms, and ran through deep forests. And always just out of reach before her ran a woman in white, whose face she could not see. Jennifer ran and ran, but the woman eluded her. Sometimes she danced with the others and sometimes she seemed to float like a vapor on the air.

By the time Jennifer awoke on the following evening, her fever had broken. She awoke from the long period of sleep to discover that she felt amazingly well. The hunger pangs were gone, and for a time she thought that she must have eaten something and simply forgotten about it. After reflection, however, she remembered reading in some book in the past that the stomach eventually shrank up and after that there were no hunger pangs. She felt if anything a little light-headed, giddy almost. And she had a plan.

She had been in old houses before. The house in which she had grown up had been an old one, in fact. And old houses had kitchens.

All houses, of course, had kitchens, but that was not

her point. The point was that old houses invariably had kitchens with doors; outside doors. The back entrance was always to and from the kitchen, or a utility room off of the kitchen.

If there was a kitchen in this house, and there had to be, there was almost sure to be a door from that kitchen to the outside. And if she could not find the kitchen from the inside, then she would find it from the outside.

It was early in the evening when she left her room to begin her search. It was not quite dark yet. She would not want to attempt finding her way about outside this house in the dark.

"That means no dawdling," she told herself firmly. Of course it also meant that once she found the kitchen she could very well choose to spend the entire night there, stuffing herself gloriously. She even smiled at the vision of herself lying on the kitchen floor, like a pet dog, chewing on an old ham bone. The thought made her mouth water.

She saw no one as she descended the stairs, but that was not, upon reflection, unusual. Judging from the hour, they were probably at their dinner. No doubt they were enjoying a sumptuous spread and laughing among themselves at her plight. Let them laugh. They would learn soon enough that she was not so helpless as they thought.

It occurred to her that she should have brought something in which to carry away a supply of food. She would need some food to take with her if she was going to escape. But now that she thought of it, there was nothing in her room that would have served the purpose. Surely she would find something in the kitchen. A basket or a paper bag even. If necessary, she would tear off her skirt and make a bundle out of it. It was far beyond salvation anyway, and modesty was at this point one of the least of her concerns.

She reached the front door without incident. So far, so good. She had a dim idea that, knowing of her increasing efforts to get away, the family might somehow try to restrain her. She would not have been surprised, upon removing the barricades from her door, to find herself locked into her room, and even now, she half-expected to find the front door locked against her.

It was not, though, nor was there any impediment outside. No one was on the lawn, nothing occurred to prevent her from following the path, as she had before, around the corner of the house. She came into the woods that pressed close against the house at the side.

This time she would not make the mistake of wandering off into the heavy growth. She knew that she might be able to find some food again, but she knew too that there was a great likelihood of getting lost, and she was determined not to do so this time; this time she had a specific destination in mind, and she meant to reach it. Regardless of how peculiar Kelsey House was, or how strangely it had been designed, the front of the house had to be joined with the rear of the house. That made sense. And to find the rear of the house, she had only to follow the walls, walking carefully, never straying from their reassuring reality. Once or twice she had to move away, to circle around some tree or patch of bushes that blocked her way, but except for those instances she remained close enough to touch the wall with one hand. In fact, she did touch it from time to time, to reassure herself. This time she was not going to get lost.

She passed window after window. At any minute she expected to see some of the family peering out, watching her. She remained afraid they would try to hinder her. But she saw no one.

She circled a small bay. There were steps beside it that led down, presumably into a cellar. At these she paused for a moment. A cellar would mean storage, perhaps of food. Should she explore here first?

No, she had started out to find the kitchen, sure now that she would succeed in doing so. If there were food in the house, and there had to be, the kitchen would be the best place to find it. She went on, only mildly curious as to what the cellar might hold.

She rounded the corner of the house finally, and she was at the rear. The growth was not so thick here, and the path began winding its way up the hill that loomed close behind the house itself. For a moment she considered following the path to determine where it led. Again she checked herself. Even assuming the path would lead her to the road eventually, or back to town, she simply could not hope to go far without food.

And there, in front of her, was the back porch;

smaller and not so pretentious, of course, as the front porch, but a porch nonetheless. And a door leading inside. Her heart pounding she mounted the wooden steps and tried the door. She almost expected to find the door locked; but it was not. It opened at her touch.

She had outsmarted them after all. This was the one idea they had not credited her with getting, the one contingency they had not blocked.

She felt filled to the brim with self-pride, and confident that success was near. A few minutes more and it would be ended, this horrible nightmarish game that they had played with her. She would have food, and here, just outside, was a path leading away from Kelsey House, leading to freedom. The freedom that would soon be hers.

She went into the kitchen. Like the rest of the house, it was filthy with dust. That much at least she had rather grown accustomed to. But dirty or not, it was a kitchen. There was a sink, a freestanding affair that was quite outdated, and there were cupboards and shelves everywhere, and an old fashioned icebox.

She stooped and opened one cupboard. Then she opened the one next to it, and the one next to that. One after the other she opened all of the lower cupboards, going around the room on her hands and knees. She stood, and opened the cupboards higher up, door after door, searching the entire kitchen.

The cupboards and shelves were filled. There were neat stacks of dishes, rows of sparkling glassware. There were pots and pans and silverware and all manner of utensils. The kitchen was complete; it held everything that could be needed in a kitchen that was designed to serve a house as large as Kelsey.

Everything, that was, except the one thing she was looking for. Everything but food. Nowhere was there a crumb of anything that might have been edible.

"A pantry," she said aloud, panting from her hurried inspection of the cupboards. Her eyes darted about the room. The back door opened directly into the kitchen. "The food is in the pantry."

She opened the first door leading from the kitchen, and found herself in the pantry. The familiar dust, the cupboards and storage one would expect in a pantry; everything was there but food.

Numb with shock, she turned and stepped back into the kitchen, to find herself facing one of the occupants of the house, one of her relatives. What was this woman's name? She saw them so seldom, she didn't remember. Helen, she thought. The woman stood in front of her, staring at her in a curious way.

"Please," Jennifer said, breaking the silence between them. "Help me. I must have food."

She was begging. She had given in, but it did not matter. She was starving. She could no longer afford her pride.

To her joy, Helen smiled, an understanding smile, and nodded. "Yes, of course," she said aloud. "Come with me."

Motioning Jennifer to follow, she led the way to yet another door. Overcome with relief, Jennifer followed her through the door.

She found herself in the dining room, and the entire family was there. They were seated at the table, eating their dinner from empty dishes, passing empty bowls and platters about the table. They looked up, all of them, as she came in, staring at her in bewildered silence, as if they could not think what she was doing here.

She felt utterly exhausted, drained not only of strength but of feeling. Without a word, Jennifer circled the table and took her place beside Mr. Kelsey, resting her hands before her on the dirty table.

The dining room. All of her efforts had brought her back to the dining room, just off the main hall. The elusive kitchen had been there all the time, adjoining the dining room, just where she should have known it would be had she been thinking clearly. And the kitchen had been as empty as the dish before her now, as empty as the trays that had been carried to her room, as empty as the path stretching before her.

She sat in frozen silence and watched them pretend to eat. For all the notice they were taking of her she might as well have remained in her room. They had returned their attention to their own dishes, and no one even looked in her direction. They seemed unaware of her presence, in fact. She watched them, lifting their forks, chewing, some of them smacking their lips with satisfaction. Aunt Abbie seemed to find something a little tough, and she chewed on it with determined vigor. Mr. Kelsey removed something, a pit perhaps, from his mouth.

The truth came to her at last. They were laughing silently and unseen, laughing at her. They had known all along that she would find the kitchen, and they had known all along she would find no food. It wasn't there, it was elsewhere, hidden somewhere in this awful, sprawling house. In another kitchen, or under some-one's bed. Somewhere where she would never find it.

CHAPTER SIXTEEN

"Jennifer?" The voice was from the hall outside, beyond the locked door.

Jennifer sat up in bed and watched the door as though expecting it to open despite the lock, and despite the dresser pushed against it. But nothing happened.

"Jennifer. It's me, Marcella."

Marcella. Strange or not the young girl was still the one friend Jennifer had at Kelsey House. And she and Wilfred were Jennifer's only hopes of escaping. She needed Marcella's help.

"Just a minute," she called back, getting up from the bed and crossing to where the dresser blocked the door. It was a laborious task, moving the heavy piece of furniture out of the way.

"Don't go," she called to Marcella, straining to push the dresser aside.

Finally the door opened sufficiently to allow Marcella to enter the room. Jennifer at once locked the door again, leaning against it as if to hold it shut against some intruder trying to get in.

"Good Heavens," Marcella exclaimed, looking at all the precautions. "Why do you want to lock your door, and put that dresser against it?"

"Because I don't feel that I'm safe here," Jennifer told her bluntly. This was no time to consider tact. Her predicament was too critical. "Marcella, you must help me. Where can I find Aunt Abbie's husband?"

"Wilfred?"

"Good Heavens," Jennifer snapped, impatient. "How many husbands does she have? Of course I mean Wilfred. I must talk to him."

"He's always in the woods this time of day," Marcella said. "Down by the stream."

Jennifer's heart sank. The woods. She would never be able to find him there without getting lost all over again; she knew what those woods were like.

As if reading her thoughts, Marcella said, "I'll take you to him if you like."

At once Jennifer's hopes flared again. "Can you?" she asked. "Would you?" Of course Marcella would know her way about the grounds. This was a stroke of luck she hadn't counted on.

"Yes, of course I will," Marcella said. "But we'll have to go now, so that I can be back in time for lunch, or Aunt Christine will be furious with me."

Jennifer wanted to suggest again that if Marcella came with her, she would avoid that sort of difficulty. But she did not want to start a delaying argument now. "We'll go at once," she said, unlocking the door quickly. "And we won't tell Aunt Christine."

But when they had left the house and started into the woods, Jennifer's courage began to pale again.

Marcella was leading the way as though she did indeed know where they were going. They had come into the woods on a path that Jennifer had not seen before. Even the very paths through the woods seemed to appear and disappear. Appear for others, disappear for her.

Marcella was little more than a child, though, and Jennifer was frightened of the woods. What if both of them ended up lost?

"Are you sure you can find your way?" Jennifer asked, increasingly uneasy as they went deeper and deeper into the forest

"Don't be afraid," Marcella assured her without even pausing. "You are, aren't you?"

"A little," Jennifer admitted.

"I know every tree here on sight. I even have names for some of them. That's old Fred there." She pointed to a particularly old, rather spindly tree.

"Isn't that a strange name for a tree?" Jennifer asked, staring at the tree. It did not look at all like a Fred to her.

"I think of them as my friends," Marcella said.

"Do you really like them? The trees, I mean. This forest?" It was difficult for Jennifer to imagine anyone liking anything about the place.

"Of course. I love everything here."

The path led up a slope. As they topped the rise, Marcella came to an abrupt halt. "There you are," she said, pointing into the distance.

Even Jennifer had to admit that the scene was a picturesque one. The stream fell from a small bluff to twist and splash its way through the hollow below. On the mossy banks ferns and cattails swayed in the gentle breeze. A willow tree dipped low over the brook, seeming to drink from the crystalline waters, and somewhere nearby a bird sang its joyful song.

At another time, under other circumstances, she might have been quite enchanted by this spot. "But this is no time for admiring the scenery," she reminded herself. There below them, sitting on a fallen log near the stream itself, was Aunt Abbie's husband, Wilfred. It was he she had come to see, and not the view.

"There he is," she said aloud, starting eagerly down the hill. She looked back impatiently to discover that Marcella had not moved from the spot.

"Well for Heaven's sake, come on," she snapped.

"I can't," Marcella said, remaining where she was. "I can't go any closer than this."

"Why on earth not?"

"This is where I drowned," Marcella said.

"Oh!" Jennifer grimaced with annoyance. She did not feel inclined just now to try to coax Marcella from her strange morbid fantasies. She looked in the direction of Wilfred, almost afraid that he would suddenly disappear from the spot. Of all the times for Marcella to be difficult, she thought.

"All right," she said to Marcella. She did not want to argue with her now. "You wait here for me. I'll only be a few minutes."

She hurried down the hill. By this time Wilfred had seen them on the path, and now he watched her approach. He did not greet her, but sat without moving. As she came closer to him, she saw that he had been whittling a piece of wood. It was a homely and harmless seeming pastime. The pen knife in his fingers moved quickly back and forth over the block, shaping it deftly and easily.

"Hello," she greeted him when she was almost to him. He met her gaze without reply. She had expected to find the customary reaction to herself in his eyes. To her surprise his expression was a different one from the one she had seen before. He did not look at all angry now, or violent. If anything, he looked rather mournfully sad, and this encouraged her a little.

"I hate to bother you," she said, since it was apparent that he was not going to return her greeting. "But I do need your help. Please, can you help me find my car? We left it in the stream, if you remember."

His answer was so long in coming that she began to think perhaps he too was speechless, like Aunt Christine's husband; but no, he had talked to her before, albeit briefly, the night of her arrival. She was about to repeat her question when he finally spoke.

"Your car's gone," he said, returning his attention to the wood in his hands.

"Gone?" she echoed. But of course, she should have foreseen that. They had stolen her purse, with the car keys in it. And they would have taken the car by this time, to prevent her escape.

"They've stolen it," she said aloud, making it a statement of fact rather than a question. He said nothing.

"Well, I don't care," she said. "They're welcome to anything, if only I can leave. Will you help me at least find the road, please? I don't care if I have to walk. I don't care if I have to crawl, if I can only leave."

He looked at her again, a long sad look. "You'll never leave here," he said finally, his voice flat and emotionless.

Jennifer was startled by his statement. It was so unlike anything he had said to her before, and it was so close to her own worst fears. "Oh, but I must," she insisted. "I must and I will. If you'll only help me, if you'll only show me where the road is...."

"I tried to leave here once," he said, plunging the knife into the wood in a deep, violent movement. The piece that he had been carving, the gentle image of a dancer, split grotesquely.

"You tried?" Jennifer asked. "But how could they stop you? They're only women, and you're a man."

"There's a curse on this place," he said. "It goes back a hundred years; no, closer to two hundred. There was a man wanted to marry one of the Kelsey girls. Her mother interfered. Refused to let them marry, and when they planned to elope, she had the girl locked up. Made her a prisoner, and hired somebody to whip the boy and run him out of town. Whoever she hired did too good a job, and the boy died from the beating he got."

He paused, looking at the broken piece of wood in his hand. It was the longest speech Jennifer had ever heard him make, and she was afraid to try to encourage him to go on, lest he stubbornly end his story there. She waited in guarded silence.

"Before he died, though, he put a curse on the Kelseys," Wilfred went on. "He said the women of the family were evil, that he saw the women of the line joined in a common bond of possession. And he cursed them and swore that they would ever remain so. He said that they will remain together for all eternity. No matter how they try to free themselves from one another. They might try to go away. They might actually live apart. And those whose lives were gentle and whose deaths were natural would find peace. But the others were forever tied together, and to this house."

Jennifer continued to sit in silence. She thought of her mother, and her possessiveness. Yes, she could see that much of it. And she could see that sort of possessiveness here, with Aunt Christine and Aunt Abbie; she could see it in their efforts to keep her here—possessiveness carried to an insane extreme.

"It's a terrible story," she said aloud, trying to dismiss her own uneasiness. "But it is only a story. A legend. And a legend can't really keep us here, if we put our minds to leaving. You and I can go, if you'll only help me...."

He wasn't listening, though; at least, he wasn't listening to her. His head was cocked as though listening to a sound in the distance, as though someone were calling him far off. He was oblivious suddenly to her presence. She held her breath, listening with him, but she heard nothing except the sighing of the wind in the trees.

He suddenly turned back to her. "You'd better go back to the house," he said. His expression was no longer sad and sympathetic, but one of fear.

"But why?" she asked. She was sure, quite sure now, that he truly wanted to help her. She had seen it in his eyes a moment before. Why had he changed so quickly, for no apparent reason?

"You'd better go," he insisted, his voice rising on a frightened note. He stood, backing slowly away from her as if she somehow were a threat to him.

Frightened herself, Jennifer moved away slightly. She wanted to argue with him, try to convince him that they could indeed leave; that she could go, and take him with her. But in some way she didn't understand she had frightened him, and his fear was contagious. What if he suddenly should become violent? He still held his carving knife in his hand, and he held it now in a menacing fashion.

"Please....," she began, but he cut her off with a violent shake of his head.

"Go," he said sharply, almost shouting.

She could do nothing but leave him there. She turned and started quickly up the rise, puzzled and frightened by this abrupt dismissal. Once she glanced back to find him staring after her, watching her go with obvious relief.

Well, she thought, perhaps it was hoping too much to think that he might be sane. No one else around the place was. Even Marcella....

She stopped in her tracks, looking about. Marcella was gone. She had reached the place where Marcella had been waiting, and the young girl was nowhere to be seen.

"Marcella?" she called. How could the girl be gone, she asked herself, annoyed and more than a little concerned. She surely had not been with Wilfred more than a few minutes, and Marcella had promised to wait for her. The child knew that she could not find her way alone through the woods. She had specifically asked Marcella to wait right here for her.

She looked back toward the stream. Wilfred too had vanished. There was no sign of him below. Like it or not, she was alone.

"And I don't like it," she said.

There was nothing she could do but start walking, watching for familiar landmarks. At least this time she had paid a little more attention to where they were going. Yes, there was the tree Marcella had pointed out earlier, the one she called Fred.

I am on the right track, she told herself, without feeling particularly reassured. At Kelsey everything could change so suddenly; one could count on nothing.

She stopped again, listening. Had she imagined it, or was there someone behind her. There was no sound now, only the gentle rustling of the leaves overhead. She started again, moving more slowly.

There it was again, the scraping of branches, the snapping of a twig. Someone was behind her, someone was following her.

"Wilfred?" she called, looking over her shoulder. She saw no one, and received no answer. The woods were silent again.

"Marcella?" Still nothing.

She began to walk again, faster now. There was no question of it, there was someone behind her, someone who stopped when she stopped, moved when she moved. It was more than sounds; she could actually feel the presence, so strongly that it was not a hunch but a certainty. She was walking faster and faster, and then she was running, and the sounds and the presence stayed close behind her, never dwindling, never falling back.

Oblivious to where she was going, Jennifer ran in panic, crashing through the brush, stumbling and rushing. Her heart pounded in her chest, her breath came in short, uneven gasps. I'm too weak for this, she thought frantically. I can't go on.

With a small groan she fell face downward upon the ground, gasping for breath. Her legs simply would not carry her any farther. Her body refused to obey her commands to flee.

Let them kill me, she thought. I haven't the strength left to fight back.

"Jennifer."

For a moment she lay with her face in the grass, trying to breathe.

"Jennifer," the voice said again, and this time she recognized the voice. She looked up.

Marcella stood over her, staring down. Marcella.

Had it been Marcella following her? She was afraid to ask. She had once again that feeling of being in a nightmare from which she must soon awaken.

She began to cry. She tried to get up, but she was too weak.

"Are you all right?" Marcella asked, kneeling beside her.

"Please," Jennifer begged in a whisper. "Help me back to the house."

A moment ago, she thought, I was begging to leave this place. And now I want to be back in Kelsey House. I too am possessed; possessed not by demons, but by the evil spirit of that house.

CHAPTER SEVENTEEN

It was the next day. At least, it seemed so to her, although her sense of time had long since abandoned her. Her fever had returned, but despite this fact, she was amazed to discover that she felt progressively stronger. Aside from her lightheadedness, she felt better than she had in several days.

But that, she reminded herself, could be a delusion. One thing was abundantly clear to her. Food or no food, assistance or no assistance, if she was to escape from Kelsey House it must be now, at once. Another day, another hour even, might be too much.

How long could a person survive without food, she wondered.

"How long," she asked aloud, "have I been in this house?" She did not know the answer to either question.

There was still one avenue of escape left open to her; she had remembered it upon waking. Still one route left unexplored.

There was a path behind the house, a path that wound its way from the house up over a hill. A path must go somewhere. Paths did not just appear, they were formed, formed by people coming and going somewhere. She would go wherever that somewhere was. There was still the question of how far she could go without food, but she did feel stronger, and there was always the possibility that she would find another house quite nearby. It would be ironic if, all this time, there were another house just over that little hill.

Again she ignored Aunt Christine's summons at her door, and waited until she thought the family would be at breakfast. This time she did not want to see any of them, not even Marcella. There was no longer any hope left in her that she could obtain any help from any of them. Marcella, Wilfred, perhaps even Mr. Kelsey— any of them might have helped her, but there was something that held them in check. She did not know what it was; something about the house, perhaps, some unknown power that was stronger than their sympathy for her. She had felt it herself, a paralyzing fear, an unseen presence that was always near, ever dangerous. It seemed a part of Kelsey House itself.

Well, she would not be paralyzed today. With quiet determination she stole from her room and from the house. This time she was in no danger of getting lost. She knew just where she was going and, in the beginning at least, she was on familiar ground. She could move quickly, following the path around the corner of the house, into the thick growth at the side. She made her way carefully along the length of the building, never straying from the wall.

She came to the rear of the house, and paused when

she reached the steps descending into the cellar of the house. Was this after all what she had been seeking? Was it possible that the kitchens they used for food preparation, and the food itself, were in the cellars? It could be only another blind alley; but the possibility was too strong to pass by without investigating.

She went down the steps slowly to the battered wooden doors. They sat at an angle, not quite horizontal in front of her. She hesitated and then reached for the handles. The doors were unlocked, and she swung them cautiously outward, half expecting cries of surprise from within. The doors moved slowly, laboriously on rusted hinges, and the only sound was the squeak of the hinges. Before her was a dark, musty interior into which the light penetrated but faintly.

"If only I had a flashlight," she thought, gazing down into that blackness. She smiled ruefully, as her own words came back to her. If she were wishing, there was a long list of things she could wish for.

It was impossible to tell what that darkness concealed. Frightened, she took a step inside.

Something moved, off to her right. Someone was hiding here, waiting for her. Or perhaps not waiting. Perhaps this was after all what she had been seeking, and they meant to frighten her away before she could confirm that fact.

I will not run away, she promised herself. I will not let them scare me again.

She took another step, and again something moved. This time it dashed out to scurry across her foot.

A rat! She shuddered with disgust, turning to run up the stairs, back into the daylight. She did not bother to close the door after herself. There was nothing there, she was sure of it. The cellar had that air of emptiness about it that she had learned to identify at Kelsey. It was better to save her strength, and her time; she would need them to make good her escape.

She came to the path; for a time she had even doubted that it would still exist. She had been half afraid that she would find that it too had vanished, that it was only something she had imagined. But it was there, inviting her up the hill.

Panting from exertion and from excitement she made her way up the hill. The path was faint in a few places, but for the most part it was easy to follow, circling about the worst of the growth.

She rounded a clump of bushes and there before her was a cemetery. It was small and old, surrounded by a wooden fence that was too low to do much more than indicate the area. It appeared to be a family plot. Jennifer paused for several seconds, curious despite her eagerness to be on. A huge elm tree shaded the place from the morning sun. The stones all of them apparently old, were haphazardly tilted, and some had fallen to the ground, victims of years of weather and neglect. The place looked little cared for, and quite desolate.

She felt an urge to look at the stones, to learn some little thing about the house and the family. She knew so little; and here was, in a sense, the family history before her. It was strange, the people in Kelsey House were the only family that she had and yet for all the time she had been here she knew no more about them than when she had first come, except that they were strange and dangerous. But there must be more to them than that. Perhaps here would be some clue to explain their behavior, to make them less bewildering to her.

She shook her head resolutely. No, this was not the time for studying family history. Fascinating though the graveyard was, it would not be of any help to her in her plan to escape. And that was where her interest lay now.

The graveyard was, she noticed, where the path led. The trail she had been following stopped at the gate in the low wooden fence.

She looked about, uncertain. She was above the house now, out of sight of it, and the hill still rose above her. Path or not, the way was open, deep with weeds but free from trees and the dense growth nearer the house. Even without the path she could not get lost here. She decided to go on to the top of the hill.

She walked more rapidly now, making her way through the tall weeds that surrounded her and finally coming over the crest of the hill. Below her was a hollow, still weedy but open and rolling; and beyond that, the woods again, standing like an ominous wall that separated Kelsey from the world beyond.

She walked more slowly, down into the hollow and then up again, although not so sharply, until she stood at the edge of the woods, the trees not so much like trees as like dark angels, hovering over her, watching her.

Here she stopped. Should she go on, commit herself to the woods and hope that she found her way through them, or perhaps follow their border as far as possible?

She was still standing, undecided, when she heard the voices. At first she thought that the occupants of Kelsey House had come after her to carry her back. She had an urge to run, to hide herself in the darkness of the woods.

But it was not them at all. Two men emerged from the woods. They were hunters, judging from the bright plaid of their jackets. Sunlight gleamed on the barrel of the rifle as they made their way nearer, following the edge of the woods.

Strangers! Outsiders! With a cry of delight she started toward them, running as fast as her weak legs would carry her. She was saved at last. The thought echoed thunderously through her brain.

They saw her when she began to run, and stopped, watching her approach. She saw them exchange glances. Their guns were tilted down toward the ground. She thought their expressions, as they watched her approach, were strange, puzzled and even a little afraid.

There was nothing for them to be afraid of, after all. But she could not help realizing, as she ran up to them, how silly the entire scene was. The logical thing to do, the thing she had an impulse to do, was to run up to them and throw herself into their arms, but somehow she could not quite picture herself doing anything so, so emotional.

Anyway, they were not holding their arms open to her. They were just standing there, staring at her in that funny way. She stopped a few feet from them, panting from the effort of running, and swayed weakly back and forth.

"Thank God you've found me," she cried breathlessly.

"Were you lost?" One of the men asked. They were older men, although nowhere near as old as Mr. Kelsey, or Wilfred. One, the one who had spoken, was gray haired, handsome in a tall gaunt way; the other was plump and had a cherubic face, round and pink.

"Yes," she said, and then, "No." She really wasn't lost this time, but how did she go about explaining that. "I've been down there, in the house. They've kept me a prisoner for days."

They followed the direction of her pointing finger and looked back at her doubtfully. But of course, she realized, they couldn't see anything from here. Kelsey House was out of sight behind the hill.

"Kelsey House," she explained, her voice rising a little. "My aunts have kept me there without any food. I've been sick, and I...I have a fever, and they took my purse...."

She was babbling rather hysterically, and she knew it, but strangely she could not make herself stop. If only they would not stare at her in that peculiar way, as though they were frightened of her. Frightened of her, for Heaven's sake? What did they think she could do?

"Kelsey House?" the short plump one repeated.

"Never heard of any Kelseys around here."

"There were, Pete," the other one said. He was speaking without looking at Jennifer. "There's a grave-yard down the woods a ways."

"The graveyard, yes," she exclaimed. At least this one knew the area. "And the house, Kelsey House."

"The house burned down thirty years ago, as I remember it," he said.

Pete, the one with the pink face, said, "Oh Lord, is that where we are?"

Burned down, Jennifer was thinking. Yes, Aunt Christine had mentioned the fire. But surely this man must know that the house was rebuilt

"The Kelseys have been around here for years," she insisted, a sense of helplessness welling up within her. They acted like they didn't believe her, like they didn't want to help her.

"I grew up around here, lady," the tall man argued, watching her intently, "and I haven't known of any Kelseys around here since I was a kid."

"Then your memory is very bad," she snapped. "The house is just over the hill there."

"Nearest place around here is Sam Williams," the one called Pete said. "About ten miles over the hollow."

Jennifer lifted a hand to her throat. Had she escaped one band of lunatics only to find another? Or was she truly out of her mind?

"Please," she said desperately. "I've been a prisoner there, I know it exists, it's as real as I am."

The tall one seemed the most sympathetic. It was he

who said, "Look, I'll tell you what. You say the house is just over that hill?"

Jennifer nodded.

"All right. We'll go up the hill and have a look."

"Ben, I don't know," the other one started to object, but Ben silenced him with a gesture.

"Only take a minute," he said decisively.

"I'll come with you," Jennifer said.

"No." His answer was quick and sharp. "You stay here. Why don't you sit down on that log there and rest, and we'll go see if we see this house you're talking about."

"Well of course you'll see it," she said petulantly. "It's there." But she did as he said, and went to the fallen log and seated herself. She was tired, and wanted to get her breath back, and if it was necessary to humor them for a few minutes, she was willing to do so. She had been humoring her "family" for days now. She had been humoring people all her life. Two minutes more couldn't matter very much.

They went up the hill. She could see them whispering to one another earnestly. It annoyed her. They were like schoolboys. They were being difficult. She would be patient.

They walked more rapidly than she had done. They came to the top of the hill. She saw them turning their heads, looking from right to left.

Now it will be over, she thought. They will come back for me, and take me away from here, and it will all be over. She closed her eyes for a moment, so tired that her head seemed to be spinning.

She opened her eyes and saw that they were still at the top of the hill. They were talking to one another, and looking back at her. They looked anxious.

The tall one called, "Look, you just stay there, okay?"

She stood up, frightened by something in their manner. "You see it, don't you?" she called back, her voice echoing through the hollow. "You see Kelsey House?"

The pause before he answered was long. "Yes, sure," he yelled a minute later. "Look, you stay there, we'll be right back."

"Don't leave me," she cried, starting to run toward them. She didn't want to be alone again, not ever.

"You stay there," the plump one cried, and when she looked, she saw that he had lifted his rifle. He had it aimed now at her.

My God, she thought, he's going to shoot me with that thing.

"You stay there," he said again, brandishing the gun menacingly.

"We're going to go down the hill and have a look at the house," the tall one said. "We'll be back later. You wait here for us."

Then they were gone, over the hill, disappeared as surely as things had disappeared at Kelsey House, and she was alone. She was frightened and bewildered. The woods near her suddenly seemed dark and threatening. She thought she heard someone or something moving in the brush. Everything seemed unreal.

Despite their instructions to remain where she was, she began to walk, and then to run, toward where they had been standing. Out of breath, she clambered to the top of the hill.

She had just a glimpse of them. They had not gone down the hill toward Kelsey House, but had circled back around, and were running. She saw them disappear into the woods down from where she had been waiting.

"Wait," she yelled, but they were gone; the woods seemed to have swallowed them up.

Running. They had been frightened of her. She thought of how she must have looked to them. Her hair was matted and tangled. She was filthy with the dust and dirt of Kelsey House, and her suit was a tattered rag. She was thin and pale, with hysteria in her eyes and her voice.

"They thought I was mad," she said aloud. "Mad or something worse."

She sank into the weeds. Maybe they were right. Maybe there was no Kelsey House. Maybe she was really mad.

But no, there it was, she could see the roof from here. Or was that an illusion too.

And if there is no Kelsey House, then there's nothing to escape from, she thought.

She was tired, very tired.

CHAPTER EIGHTEEN

Ben Lester was not a cowardly man. Granted, the woman that he and Pete Davis met in the woods was an odd one. He had to agree she looked like a wild woman, like she was touched in the head. She was dirty and unkempt; but it wasn't just that. It was the wild look in her eyes and the way she kept waving her hands, and jabbering away about things that didn't make any sense. She was enough to unnerve anybody, he had to admit that.

Still, there was something about her that bothered him, something almost sad, but not quite. He tried to express his opinion to Pete.

"She looked, I don't know, sad," he said.

"Sad my eye," Pete replied, hurrying on as fast as his short thick legs would manage. "She's like nothing I ever saw before or want to see again. Crazy at the very least. No sir, I ain't going back there now or ever. I'm going to get me in my car and start for home, and you can come along if you want to or you can stay behind and walk back by yourself, it's all the same to me, but I won't wait for you." In the end Ben had given in to Pete's feelings on the matter. They had climbed into Pete's old Buick and Pete had driven home, faster than was his usual style. But the incident stayed on Ben's mind.

Later that evening, sitting in front of the fireplace, Ben discussed the matter with his wife, and hinted for her to say if he had done the right thing or the wrong thing by leaving that woman there.

"I suppose Pete was right about her being crazy," he told his wife. "She was a strange-looking thing, that's the truth."

His wife was a short, pink creature, once rather pretty, although she had grown too plump too fast. She was working now at her mending, her hands moving rapidly and skillfully over one of her husband's shirts. She only nodded her head silently, meaning, to her husband, that she had not yet made up her mind just what she did think about the incident, and was still considering it.

"Wonder where she came from?" he mused.

"If she was even real," she said. She glanced at him once over the rim of her glasses, and then looked back at her sewing.

"You think I was seeing things?" he asked. He was trying out this suggestion, rolling it around like a taste of something new on his tongue.

"There's been a lot of stories about that land over the years," she said, not answering him directly. "You and Pete ain't the first two to say you saw people out that way. Not two years ago Joe Clyne's wife told me that Joe said he saw a whole flock of them out there, dressed funny and kind of dancing around in the weeds. She said she thought Joe was going crazy, but I said there's no accounting for all the things in this world. There's stranger things, as the good book says, than is told of."

"That's true," he said, puffing on his pipe. He tilted his chair back so that it was resting on just two legs. "Most folks shy away from that place altogether. Why, I don't think there's a one of the men that hunts as close to it as Pete and me. Seems a shame too. It's good hunting up there."

Neither of them spoke for a moment, and the silence was broken only by the sound of a log settling on the fire.

"Funny thing," Ben said a little later. "The way she kept talking about that old Kelsey House. That's what made me realize she wasn't right in the head, talking about that old place, and it not standing all these years. You know, I stood there and watched it the day it burned. Not a timber left standing that was worth anything but kindling."

"Good land, they used to say." His wife was noncommittal.

"That it is," he said. "My old man talked for a time about buying it, but it all went to some relative in some other part of the state. He wrote to her, but he never got an answer. Figured maybe she was going to rebuild the house or something. But whatever she wanted it for, she never got around to it, I guess, and never put it up for sale. My dad finally stopped writing to her. Then when the stories started around about it, I guess everybody lost interest in wanting it."

"Just as well it worked out that way," she said. She had finished sewing on the pocket that had been torn loose from her husband's shirt. She held it up to inspect it with a critical eye.

"Guess you're right," he said. "Wouldn't want it now, with a bad name hanging over it." He thought for a moment before saying, "Good hunting up there, though."

She bit the end of a thread loose. "I'd say you and Pete ought to find yourselves another spot for your hunting. Doesn't seem right to me, meeting strangers way out there in the middle of nothing. Even if she was for real, what was she doing out there? There'd have to be something odd about her, wouldn't there?"

She began to gather her sewing gear together, returning everything neatly to its place in the sewing box on the floor beside her. "As for myself, I don't think I'll even say anything about it to anyone," she said. "Knowing Josie Davis, I don't guess it'll stay a secret, but I don't want any credit myself for spreading that kind of tale. Let someone else do it, I say."

Ben slept easily that night.

CHAPTER NINETEEN

The graveyard was larger than she remembered it. The stones were closer together than was usual, crowding quite a number of graves into the area enclosed within the fence. Jennifer made her way carefully about the stones, trying to avoid stepping on what she thought might be a grave; that was bad luck, or so she remembered from her childhood.

She did not know just why she had come back here, except that she had a sense of utter futility about everything else. Here at least was a sense of peace and calm. Ironically, though, that tranquility came not from freedom, as one might suppose, but from captivity. From here there was no escape, and its very certainty made you feel at ease with it.

It had been like that with her mother and herself. She had been confined within the strong walls of her mother's personality, and within those confines, she had been calm; not happy, perhaps, but without the confusion that attends the illusion of freedom. And it had been an illusion. She had thought herself free with her mother's death. But in fact she was more confined than before. Without her mother's strong will to guide her, she had been confined by her own ignorance and fear, confined by her mistakes, confined by her longing for love and acceptance. She was trapped here, at Kelsey House, and yet there were no walls, no weapons had been raised against her. No one had spoken less than lovingly to her.

She looked at the grave markers about her. The names inscribed upon them meant nothing to her. If she knew more about the family history, she might be able to identify some of them, but as it was, they were only so many names cut into stone. Names of people who were, in some way or another, relatives of hers. A family. All of her life she had wanted a family, like other people had, with aunts and cousins and grandparents. And here it was: the strange people at Kelsey House, and the rotting graves around her. These were her family.

She was about to leave the graveyard; it had no meaning to her. But one name caught her eye, and she stooped to see the stone more clearly.

Marcella Brandon, it said. An aunt, obviously, some distant relative for whom the Marcella she knew had been named.

She scraped away a covering of dirt and moss to read the rest of the inscription:

Born 1850
Died 1865

She had died at the age of fifteen; how tragic that sounded. Fifteen. That was Marcella's age now, the live Marcella.

Her thoughts went to the girl in the house. This, of course, was where that Marcella had gotten her strange notions about herself. She was fifteen, and she was named for another Marcella who had died when she was fifteen. It was a striking coincidence, one that would easily spark the imagination of an impressionable young girl.

Jennifer guessed, even before she had scraped away some more moss and read the rest of the marker, that the first Marcella had drowned. She stared at those words for a long time, trying to ignore the awful thought that came unbidden into her mind. She closed her eyes and shook her head, as if she could dislodge that thought, but it held fast to her consciousness.

Something flashed before her eyes, a memory of her mother reading a letter. She had learned of the death of Aunt Lydia. Aunt Lydia had died in some way too violent or unpleasant to explain to a child of Jennifer's age.

"We had hoped Lydia would be with us, but she was delayed," Aunt Christine had said. "She'll join us in a little while."

Surely that must be another Lydia. After all, there could be two Lydias in one family, just as there were two Marcellas.

Half walking, half crawling, she clambered to the next stone and began to rub away the dirt and moss that covered the inscription. Christine Kelsey. Died, 1829.

The one next to that was Abbie Longworth, who died in 1870.

"God in Heaven," Jennifer whispered, staring at the stones around her. They were all here, all of them. There was a large stone for Helen and Maggie Kelsey, who had died, the stone said, in the burning of Kelsey House.

Kelsey House. A house that wasn't there, and people in it who ate no food, needed no clothing, or cars, or cleaning....

But Kelsey House was there. She had lived in it for days, she had walked on the wooden floors, opened and closed doors, touched its walls.

"Those who went—naturally never returned...." No, that was not the way Aunt Christine had said it. She had said, "Those who went *naturally*—never returned...."

"A curse on the house...women of the line joined in a common bond of possession...they will remain together for all eternity...."

Women...possession...together for all eternity.

Suddenly she knew. She knew the truth about Kelsey House, and its inhabitants. She knew that Kelsey was not here, not really, not so that ordinary people could see it. Nor were the inhabitants. They were dead, all of them, spirits. Echoes of what had once been life, echoes sounding through the corridors of time.

But she knew more even than that. She knew the identity of that other woman, the house guest she had not yet seen face to face, the mysterious visitor to her room, the one who followed her about, called her name, comforted her when she cried.

"But she went naturally," she argued with herself, speaking aloud.

Or had she? Jennifer thought again of that fateful night, and the voice that had called her name; the voice that grew weaker and weaker.

Her heart pounding, she ran from the graveyard, down the path, circling the house without touching it. She must see someone, talk to them, demand the truth. They must see that she herself was not dead, that she was alive, and so she had no place here at Kelsey.

"I'm not dead," she sobbed, scarcely coherent. "I'm not dead."

She came to the front of the house, along its length, to the steps that led up to the entrance. And there she stopped, looking up with horror at the woman on the porch, watching her.

There was no doubt that it was Elenora Rand. The frown was the same frown Jennifer remembered, the frown that had given her such fear as a child. It was, beyond any question, her mother frowning at her, starting down the steps toward her in that same authoritative way she always had.

"No," Jennifer said, her voice hoarse. She stared with wide, wild eyes, and shook her head, and tried to back away. "No, it isn't true. I didn't hear you call. I was asleep. I dreamed your voice. I didn't want you to die. I didn't kill you. I didn't hear you call."

Her voice rose on each phrase, until she was screaming. Then in a panic she whirled about and began to run blindly. She did not even see the lawn she crossed, nor the woods as she entered them. Whether she was being pursued or not, she did not know. Certainly her own terror ran behind her, nipping at her like a savage beast. She was ignorant of the branches that reached out to scratch her and hold her back, ignorant of the frightened cry of a jay as he fled before her.

She reached the creek, splashing into the shallow water. The creek. The chill of the water brought her a moment of sanity, set her mind to reasoning again. She hardly slowed in her flight as she turned and ran with the water. The creek crossed the road, crossed it at the spot where she had left her car. If she followed the water, it would lead her to the road, and away from Kelsey House. When she had found the road, she would run until she was so far they would never catch her. They would never bring her again to Kelsey House. She would die first.

"You'll never leave here." The statement rang in her ears.

"I will," she shouted aloud, drowning out the remembered voice. "I will leave! I will!"

She ran with the water, gasping and panting, ignoring the leaden weight that grew in her limbs, and the ache in her chest that became a fire. She went on through the cold, rushing stream, stumbling and slipping, until her foot caught beneath a slime-covered rock and she fell, half in, half out of the water.

Her ankle was broken. She knew it the moment she tried to pull her leg free. She tried to crawl, but her strength was gone. She lay in a crumpled heap, heaving and sobbing and gasping for breath. Her body was in the water, and her head on the mossy bank, and she cried and thought of Marcella, drowning in the stream.

But she was not going to drown. She would lie here, the cold water running over her body, until she died from the exposure, or until they found her.

Her tortured mind could bear no more, and she sank into a welcome unconsciousness.

Her breathing slowed, coming more naturally.

The stream flowed over her.

She woke, and was still trapped. She tried to free herself, but her foot was caught and she hadn't the strength to move it. She cried, and she screamed, until her throat had gone dry and her voice was only a whisper.

She slept again, and the stream flowed.

The day became night. All around her the earth lay still and no living person stirred. There were glimpses of stars overhead, and after a time, something brighter that might have been the sun. Or might not have been. For a time she ached with a dull pain that went all through her; in time, even that faded. She felt nothing. She was still and motionless, and looked as if she might only be waiting for someone to come.

Night again. Cold water rushing over her.

There were faces, glimpses of faces close to her own, and voices, and snatches of conversation. She heard

"Exposure," and "Pneumonia," and "Malnutrition." They had called in a doctor, of course.

She tried to talk, to explain. "Help me," she begged, writhing and twisting upon her bed. "They're trying to kill me. They want me to die. Help me."

"...crazy," someone was saying. "Where'd you find her, Ben?"

The word went spiraling through her consciousness, downward, carrying her deep into herself: crazy, crazy, crazy. Around and around it went, like a corkscrew, and her mind followed it, turning in and down. It was darker than she had ever seen before.

Then there was music, sweet unfamiliar sounds that seemed to fill not only her ears but her very being. And colors—no patterns or designs, but only colors, hues and tints that she had never before seen nor imagined, beautiful colors filling everything. And light, parting the darkness, seeming to sear her eyes.

Light, and color.

CHAPTER TWENTY

She woke to find her room bathed in sunlight. She yawned, stretching her arms high over her head, and realized that she felt wonderful. Her body seemed to be weightless, as if every care and strain had been lifted from her. She could not remember ever feeling so alive. And the room, how sparkling it was, how vivid the paper flowers that covered the ceilings and walls. And everything seemed freshly washed with sunlight.

At the dresser, Aunt Abbie was busily arranging fresh flowers in the little vase.

"Good morning," Abbie greeted her with a cheery smile. "I hope you slept well."

"Yes, I did," Jennifer replied. "And it is a good morning, isn't it?"

"I didn't disturb you, did I?" Abbie looked concerned for a moment, but Jennifer's smile reassured her.

"I think nothing could disturb me this morning," she said with a laugh.

Abbie looked pleased. She gave her flowers a final pat. "I think the roses get prettier every day," she said, admiring her own efforts.

"They really are quite beautiful this morning,"

Jennifer agreed. And it was true. The roses were the loveliest she had ever seen. The reds were like the color of blood, and the pinks like the glow of a summer sunset.

"Thank you," Abbie said. She started for the door. "Oh, and breakfast is ready."

When she had gone, Jennifer rose from the bed. She slipped into the white robe Aunt Abbie had left for her. The fit was perfect, and it felt, as she walked, as though she were truly floating on air. The robe billowed gracefully behind her as she descended the stairs.

The family all looked and smiled as she entered the dining room. How pleasant it was to be among one's own! Without asking, she seated herself in the empty chair beside her mother.

"I hope you slept well dear," her mother greeted her, patting one of Jennifer's hands in the affectionate and possessive gesture Jennifer remembered from the past.

"Oh, yes," Jennifer said. "And I'm starving."

Her mother smiled slightly at that, the same stiff smile of old.

"Well, this should help a bit," Aunt Christine suggested, handing her a large platter of steaming biscuits. "We've eggs, and fresh cream, and fruit this morning. So eat heartily."

It was, Jennifer had to admit, a delicious breakfast, and she helped herself generously. Everything looked and smelled wonderful, and tasted just as good. She began to devour her food greedily.

Glancing to her left, she saw Marcella. Marcella sat

without touching the plate before her. Jennifer looked toward Aunt Christine and raised one eyebrow quizzically.

"Oh, that Marcella," Aunt Christine laughed, seeing the glance and the raised eyebrow. "You know, in all these years, I've never been able to coax her to eat breakfast."

"I don't like breakfast," Marcella said flatly.

"I just don't know what will become of that girl," Aunt Christine said.

ABOUT THE AUTHOR

V. J. BANIS is the critically acclaimed author ("the master's touch in storytelling..."—*Publishers Weekly*) of more than 200 published books and numerous short stories in a career spanning nearly a half century. A native of Ohio and a longtime Californian, he lives and writes now in West Virginia's beautiful Blue Ridge.

You can visit him at http://www.vjbanis.com

www.ingramcontent.com/pod-product-compliance
Lightning Source LLC
Chambersburg PA
CBHW031423250626
47155CB00004B/1603